EDGED IN PURPLE

A NOVEL

JOHN W. FEIST

Cover Design: Miladinka Milic
Page Design & Typesetting: Domini Dragoone

Publisher's Catalog-in-Publication Data:

Names: Feist, John W., author.
Title: Edged in Purple: a novel / John W. Feist.
Description: Falls Church, VA : Winter Wheat Press, [2024]
Identifiers: ISBN: 979-8-9904300-0-6 (print) | 979-8-9904300-1-3 (ebook)
Subjects: LCSH: Orestes, King of Argos (Mythological character)--Fiction. | Man-woman relationships-- Fiction. | Royal houses--Fiction. | Time travel--Fiction. | LCGFT: Romance fiction. | Mythological fiction. | BISAC: FICTION / Fairy Tales, Folk Tales, Legends & Mythology. | FICTION / Literary. | FICTION / Romance / Fantasy.
Classification: LCC: PS3606.E378 E34 2024 | DDC: 813/.6--dc23

PUBLISHED BY

EDGED IN PURPLE

The Edge

CHAPTER ONE

When my wife, Thetis, and I lost our son in the war, she wanted to die, but she couldn't of course—not a goddess. She could hurt, but not die, ever. I could die at a moment's notice. Sadly, in my case, with no heir.

Thetis could talk to Zeus and could always get him to listen. Zeus knew what had happened to Achilles and knew that her heart would always hurt because of it. He listened until she ran out of things to say. Mostly what she said was how we should never have let him go to war in the first place. That guilt stung her deeply. She wanted to die because of that; she wanted it more than anything else. She *could* have anything else, but not that.

You've heard of Zeus but perhaps not of Thetis. She is a nymph of the sea, a Nereid, one of fifty.

In the society of Olympian gods, Thetis married beneath her rank since I was a mortal. It didn't matter that I was King Peleus, hero of Thessaly. I've always understood that Zeus is fond of her. Since that's something I can't change, I put up with it. Besides, I had my own baggage: a bad starter marriage, and a wild goose chase that took me to sea, which is where I first saw Thetis.

Zeus generously set us up in this sheep operation. We call the place the Fold. It had been vacant for years. We got it up and running again. We didn't have any more children of our own after that. We got a lot of visitors, though. That's one of the special aspects of the Fold.

Have you ever wondered what it'd be like to be raised by shepherds? Maybe when you're reading along, absorbed in a story, and some kid is sent to "live with shepherds" or maybe just comes from a place where there are shepherds. *What goes on there and who are these shepherds?*, you're wondering, of course. It's a good thing you do. If no one ever wondered about it, nothing would ever happen there. It absolutely must happen!

We get visitors to the Fold from all kinds of stories, from diverse times, places, and lineage. They descend on us from storytellers who put them out to pasture for a bit, in the care of shepherds. We keep them until the time comes for them to go back to their stories. Their storytellers have their fates already planned out on a roadmap. After all, the Latin word for fate, *fatum*, means "that which has been spoken."

But what if one of the storybook characters isn't content with his storyteller's roadmap? What if he'd want to choose a different direction for himself? That's the one who showed up in the middle of the night about a month ago. We'd never had anyone quite like him before.

This story is about him and the people who went with him.

HE WAS SIXTEEN YEARS old when he appeared at the Fold. He wore a thorn-ripped tunic edged in purple. He stood five feet five inches tall in his sandals, deeply tanned, and muscular. His head was covered in dark brown, wiry hair that wound around itself into short, thick curls we came to compare to tortellini. His eyes, the color of nutmeg, seemed to produce, not reflect, light. His long, straight nose ended in a tip that drooped over sprouts of a mossy mustache. His legs were marked everywhere by battles with field stubble, wild berry thorns, and the raspy undersides of forest ferns. He had foraged and slept rough over the entire seven hundred miles between here and his festered home. He was a royal. I knew his family; it's a messy story.

He took to sleeping in the barn loft. Heh, no not alone. She was also sixteen—been with us since she was a baby. We raised her as our daughter. I saw them go up there. You don't need divine foresight to figure it out.

They first met in the kitchen the morning after he got here. She was slicing figs on the dough board. He came to the doorway looking for one of his belongings, but saw her instead. He just stood there looking at her. Her long, black hair with rust-colored highlights was gathered into a two-layered bun, away from her high forehead and trim eyebrows. The oval of her face ended in a narrow chin below a smile on full lips. She was tapping one clogged foot and humming intimately. Her cotton housedress, dyed in a bath of blueberries, was tied with a white sash. Its skirt fell below her knees over tanned calves.

Thetis was upstairs washing her ankle-length hair. Her strong, underwater voice shattered the silence: "Rise and shine! Rise and shine! Cold front moving in with scattered showers."

He said, "How does she know?"

She said, "She's a goddess, she foresees. You're new. You'll see."

He stepped to the table where she stood and picked up a piece of fig. "I'm not at all new, I'm from an ancient family in Mycenae." He chewed and gulped the fruit hurriedly.

She slid her bleached elm cutting board out of his reach and turned away. "New here, I mean. Who are you?"

"Orestes."

Reaching into the rush-woven basket on the floor for another fig, she said, "Arrested? I'm sorry. I know the feeling; I was born in a prison." Sunlit sparkles flashed from her eyes as she glanced back with a smile.

"It's *Orestes*." His eyes met hers. "Who are you?"

She shrugged and handed him another piece of fig. "I'm Lost."

Their fingers touched as he accepted it. "I think I'm lost, too."

"No, my name is Perdita. I hate my name. It's Latin. It means 'lost.'"

He said, "It's an uncommon name."

Frowning, "I want to be uncommon but to have a common name."

"All right, let's choose another name for you."

"Don't be weird," she said, as she turned away. "I like what I see of you, but I don't want you to be weird. You can't un-choose your given name."

Orestes cocked his head. "Of course you can." He sniffed. "This kitchen—it's so different from the one at home. That hearth is wider than a spear! The bacon smells wonderful. You're cooking it on that new, black metal. We only use that to shoe chariot horses. We use copper in the kitchen. I haven't eaten since yesterday noon."

Perdita gracefully scooped the fig pieces into a thickly potted glazed crock the color of brown butter to join the compote of quinces, cherries, and plums. "You're not lost, you were sent away. All of us got here that way. You were taken in by these shepherds. They took me in, too, after Daddy beached me down-river at high tide."

He swallowed. "What time is breakfast?"

"After you milk the goats. Be careful, she's coming this way."

Thetis swept in and the scent of seaweed on sunbaked sand joined the kitchen smells. "Orestes, isn't it? Arrived late last night. Did you sleep well?"

Orestes stared at the woman before him in her shimmering, flowing aqua dressing gown. Her iridescent arms and hands floated slightly away from her hips; copper bracelets banded loosely around her wrists. Her commanding presence seemed to lengthen her four feet, nine-inch height. Her neck and wide shoulders were thick and muscular, as were her thighs and calves, a physique developed from long-distance swimming with dolphins. Her eyelids blinked from bottom up over clear, roseate eyes.

"Thank you for asking, I slept off and on. I won't be staying long."

"Yes, you will, for about a month." Wrinkling her nose, "Just the fruit for me, Perdita. Can you help him find some work clothes?"

"Yes, ma'am."

Thetis smiled. "Helpful girl. You'd make a perfect lady-in-waiting. You'll like Orestes, he's handsome, as you can see, and earnest. Wish he were mine, in a way. Not that I'd want to be his mother. Won't go there." She turned to go and stopped. "Perdita, before I forget it, I need to teach you something."

"What thing?"

"Sex."

Perdita's brows pinched studiously, "Will you teach it to both of us?"

Turning back, she stifled a laugh. "Just you. You're to be betrothed to the Prince of Bohemia." She nodded toward Orestes, "Him? We'll have to see."

Perdita was stunned. She had only met the Prince of Bohemia once and she had little interest. "When?" she said.

Thetis said, "Much later in your story." The air whispered crisply as she left. Somewhere a wren rasped a long scold.

"I already know about sex," Orestes said brightly.

Perdita shook her head, "No, you don't, not yet. She said 'we'll have to see' about you. What size trousers do you take?"

"I dunno. I've only ever worn a white tunic with purple trim. If you want to know about sex, how 'bout after the milking?"

Perdita set places at the long table under the windows opposite the hearth. "Then comes breakfast."

Orestes moved a bench to the table. "Breakfast is best after sex."

She stopped and looked at him askance. "How did you learn about sex?"

Orestes started to smile but suddenly his knees weakened. He steadied himself but his head throbbed. He looked up and muttered, "My sister!"

Alarmed, "She taught you…?"

"No, not about that." He looked around suddenly, his eyes wide with fright. "I'm afraid for my sister. Something's happened to her. Something just flashed in my head. I can't explain it."

"You should ask Thetis. She—"

"Foresees, yes, you said. I had a feeling just then. It's gone now."

Perdita said, "I've always wanted a sister. I'm an only child in an accidental family. The shepherds are nice. I think my mother was. I can't think my father was—he condemned me to death. I'm lucky to be here at all."

"Families can be complicated," Orestes said. "I've been betrothed, too."

Perdita began humming again, only louder and tunelessly. She stood straight, frowning. "Is she pretty? Your fiancée?"

"I was only four when I was told."

"And she?"

"Eleven. I liked her name. Growing up I came to think she was pretty. You remind me of her. You are beautiful. I thought you and I could have—"

"Yes?"

"Breakfast. Together. Before and after."

"Betrothed?" Perdita laid the last pewter plate on the table with a firm thud, eyebrows arched. "Who?"

"Hermione. She's family."

Perdita whirled to face him. She stamped her foot. "Mother!"

"Cousin actually; Aunt Helen's daughter."

Perdita gripped his shoulders and shook him once, hard. "No, my mother. Hermione's *my* mother. In Sicily, in jail. Here, I have her indictment—it's from a play that came out in London." She went to the cupboard where she kept the quarto-sized bound book. She opened it and read:

Hermione, queen to the worthy
Leontes, King of Sicilia, thou art here accused and
arraigned of high treason, in committing adultery
with Polixenes, King of Bohemia.

Orestes gasped. "What happened?"

"She denied it, which didn't help. She said:

If powers divine behold our human actions
I doubt not then but innocence shall make
False accusation blush and tyranny
Tremble at patience.

"'Tyranny tremble at patience.' That's beautiful. Where did you get that…what is it?"

Perdita smiled as she replaced the slim book on its cupboard shelf. "It's from a play. I've only read the first act. It's in this book that Thetis lent to me. She has all the books ever written."

"What's a book?"

Just then Thetis and I came down for breakfast. We couldn't help overhearing them. Perdita was puzzled by his question. I explained that he had learned from papyrus scrolls and storytelling, just like I did at his age. That seemed to satisfy her about the books, but she was still stirred up about the other.

She said, "Orestes, I'd like for us to get off on the right foot, but you startled me with talk of marrying my mother. Just who are you? Where are you going?"

"Perdita, believe me, I'm not going to marry your mother. I come from Argos and my family rules Mycenae. I've asked myself the same question, 'where am I going?' I know that before I left home, I was going to war, absolutely. I trained for the hunt and for war. If I were at home, when I turn eighteen, I'd become a cadet. Then, after two years of that I'd be deployed to the front, in Troy. That's standard there. What is not exactly standard about me is that I am heir to Father's throne. My sister, Electra, sent me away as soon as he left for the war. My cousin was coming to live with Mother. Electra wanted me out of reach of his unsafe mix of ambition and bad temper, one of the reasons I love her. I'm homesick for her and my other sisters, Iphigenia and Chrysothemis, and my father, of course. Not so much my mother. War is my family's pathway to wealth. Where I come from, people value flashy wealth and power. My father taught me that fine silks, gold, and war loot measure status and honor."

"Is that what *you* want?" asked Perdita.

Orestes looked at Perdita and touched his fingertips to her temple to push aside a spill of hair. "Not so much anymore."

Perdita bent her head slightly against his hand. It was quiet in the kitchen.

Thetis broke in. "You hear that sound? That's the goats that you're not milking."

"I haven't had breakfast. I'm a royal. Besides, I really need to find something I've misplaced."

"The goats don't care. Perdita, take him to the barn."

Perdita looked up with a smile, "Is there fresh hay in the loft?"

"Yes, there is," I said.

"Let's go, Orestes," said Perdita, giggling.

Sure enough, it started raining.

CHAPTER TWO

They seemed real happy right from that first day, although the very next day, Orestes was out of sorts at breakfast. He tapped me on the shoulder after we'd eaten and tipped his head toward the door. I followed him into the crisp, breezy air. He ran his fingers through his tangled hair and hemmed and hawed. I told him he could talk plainly to me.

"King Peleus, this is a terrible thing to have to admit, but I did something stupid, and I need your help."

The boy was in distress. So, I just tried to reassure him that he could talk openly to me. I figured it had something to do with the hayloft the day before. I was wrong. Eventually he came out with it.

"I lost my *xiphos*."

"Your *sword*?"

"Un huh."

I knew what a Spartan cadet is taught about his *xiphos*, the short fighting blade, wide in the middle, tapering to a sharp point at the business end. Every soldier considers it part of his own body. I know he was taught never to give up his sword, just as he was taught to return from battle either with his shield or on it. Implied in all that training must be the mandate to not just lose the thing. I said, "Any idea where? Where were you the last time you had it?"

"Now I remember. It was at the spot where I came into this place you call the Fold. But it was dark, and I don't know the way back. Would you please take me there to help me find it?"

"Of course!" I said. "It'll give us a chance to show you around the place. Let me go get Perdita."

"Please, I'd rather she not know about this."

"Orestes, since this time yesterday, Perdita has gotten to know quite a bit about you, wouldn't you say? It's fine, don't worry about your pride. I have a notion where the sword is. It's in a safe place. We don't have any need for arms and such. We live peaceful lives and so do the rest of the shepherd families. Perdita has no background in swords or war so to her it'd be like misplacing a shovel. She'll want to take a picnic."

"But," he said, "I am humiliated, and I don't want her to see me this way. I didn't want to say anything about it yesterday. I was just getting to know her and the milking. And the hay."

"Perdita sees people very clearly for who they are, Orestes. This is a loving family we've built here. We don't have the same notions of pride or rank you grew up with. If you don't want her to see you in humiliation, then shed it. Treat this as just another day on the ranch. That much is in your control. Make the most of it. You go see to your chores and I'll have a word with Perdita."

Perdita was practical after I explained things. She said, "Why not just ask Thetis? She'll know."

"Come on, Perdita," I said, "This is a chance to show him around and get out and about. Thetis probably does know, but her mind gets tired of the trivia she foresees. We'll be back mid-afternoon."

"Shall I pack a lunch?"

I smiled and said, "I thought you'd never ask."

So, off we went, the three of us. I led us toward the Edge. They started out holding hands. *Some Spartan*, I thought.

"This place doesn't look like my country or anywhere else I've been," he said as he looked around.

Perdita said, "It's all I've ever known. I love the colors."

"It's like a rainbow," he said.

"Everything except our home is like that," she said. "See, things are colored red, yellow, or blue, like that chestnut tree. And some things are a vivid pastel, like the aspen grove we're coming to."

"But not your cottage," he interrupted. "It's whiter, like buttermilk, and the edges not quite red."

"Yes," she said, clasping his forearm. "You are right! It's like the bark of a cedar tree."

"It's big for a cottage."

She nodded, "The bedrooms can take twenty immigrants when we're full."

The Fold looked more like a painting or a stage set. The barn and everything, even the ancient chestnut trees, were like stiff cut-outs, edged in black. The Fold was invisible to the rest of the world, a crease in time. It was a blissful, green, enclave of foothills bounded by the Edge on the east side and the Other Edge on the west side. To go over the Edge was to go into the time of the story you came from. To go over the Other Edge...I have no idea. No one had ever done it. Thetis said to stay away from it, and I did.

I keep a few sheepdogs. The sounds of the dogs and the bells we put on the lead sheep tell you where the herd is grazing. Their sounds carry, but sometimes they can get out of earshot, like that day we went back for the sword. Perdita was in no hurry. I've been out in the fields with her many times and she's usually all business. That day it was amusing—she'd go five or six steps, stop, let go of Orestes' hand, and drop down to examine an alpine flower. She didn't pick it, just examined it, as if she'd never seen one before in all her sixteen years.

"This is lupin," she said. Orestes squatted down beside her. "When it blooms, later, in the spring, it will have deep blue, tiny flower petals. It will cover entire hillsides."

Orestes touched the tiny plant. "I look forward to seeing it that way. Right now, don't you think we should keep moving?"

It was charming but it slowed us down. After a bit, he broke away and went ahead where he turned back with his hands on his hips. Perdita did not take the hint.

I said, "It's not like you to keep stopping like this."

She said, "These little flowers are ten times prettier and more interesting than any sword. I'm hoping he'll stop thinking about his sword so much."

After that, he took her hand again and stopped when she did. He'd bend over to see what she was looking at.

I despaired of getting to the Edge and back in one day. I thought a makeshift overnight camp under the stars would add a nice touch to their flirtatious mood, but then I thought again: this is winter, after all. So, I walked past them and picked up my pace without saying a word. Sure enough, they soon caught up with me.

We crested a hillock of clover and brittle stalks of wildflowers that had finished for the season, and there it was, looming in front of us.

The best way to think of what the Edge looked like is to think about standing in the wings of a stage, right on the apron behind its proscenium arch. You'd first see some narrow curtains that recede upstage from the main curtain. There were ropes and pulleys that adjust the curtains and fly set sections if that's what's called for. There was a huge light panel capable of magnificent visual effects. Across from that was a long (really long) prop table. The main curtain was up that day. Dropped behind it was a scrim—a flat, tightly stretched, gauzy, light curtain that can either allow what's onstage to be seen through, or, if front-lit, shows what's been painted on the front of the scrim, but nothing behind it. That's what Orestes saw two nights ago when he stumbled through the bracken, looking for game. To him, from that angle, the space ahead of him looked exactly like the rest of the forest. As he hacked his way forward, his sword tip rent the scrim and in he slipped through the opening. Where there'd normally be a stage was an upsloping field of clover, like so much of the rest of the Fold.

Orestes was aghast as he looked around. "What is this place? It looked so different two nights ago."

I said, "It's something like the fourth wall on a stage between actor and audience."

Orestes looked at Perdita in amazement. "I don't understand a word he just said. Do you?"

I spoke up. "Yesterday you asked what a 'book' is and I said it's like the scrolls you were used to. Well, this is the same thing but applied to plays. You went to an amphitheater at a festival to see a play in your time. It's the same as that, only with more equipment."

Orestes said, "I've seen a lot of plays at the Acropolis in Tiryns. I used to make stuff up and pretend I was an actor." He stepped to the center of the clover slope, put one fist on his hip and raised his other over his head.

> ORESTES: *Bonehead Heracles, I'm stronger than you by*
> *ten times!*

Perdita laughed and skipped out on the slope beside him, forearm pressed against her brow.

> PERDITA: *Orestes, Orestes, wherefore art thou Orestes?*
> ORESTES: *I'm about to teach this man a lesson!*
> PERDITA: *The head of bone lies on thine own spine!*
> *Will you never learn to use your brain*
> *And save uncalloused hands for holding mine?*
> PELEUS: *Leave off forsooth, for soon*
> *We needs must head back south*
> *To featherbeds and mull-ed wine.*

Perdita crossed downstage right. "Over here, Orestes. Here's your *xiphos*, on the prop table."

The prop table held all kinds of things besides his sword: a red riding hood, a long, exquisite rose made of gleaming silver, a soldier's wife's handkerchief, a simple sling shot, a trumpet, a basket of woven rushes, a skull, a glass slipper, and a long section just of cradle boards. Everything had been placed there with great care.

Orestes stumbled forward, still craning his neck to try to take everything in. He reached for his sword.

"No!" I shouted. Perdita grasped his wrist.

"Never touch anything on the prop table until it's your time to go on, to go back," I explained.

"I don't understand," he stammered.

Perdita spoke softly, "It'll take a while to get used to, Orestes. There is no hurry. I'm going to be beside you from now on. I'll explain as best I can."

"Did you bring the mending kit?" I asked.

"Yes, of course," she said.

I said, "We should fix the scrim and start back if we expect to get home before dark."

Orestes asked, "You knew all along where my sword was?"

I shrugged, "I had a hunch. It happens occasionally. We never know exactly when or how a visitor will drop into the Fold. It wasn't hard to figure out. You have a bite of picnic lunch. Perdita and I need to tend to our mending."

Orestes said to Perdita, "I feel really lost now. So, I know how you feel."

She touched his cheek and said, "You just have to start thinking a little differently is all. It'll come. I'll help. I really want to help. I'm really, really glad you fell into the Fold. I'm starting to feel a purpose of my own."

Before we left, Orestes went back to the prop table for a last look at his sword. It rested next to a golden apple. He turned his attention to the apple.

"What's this?" he asked as he leaned over to examine it closer.

"I wouldn't get too close to that," I said.

Perdita joined him and stared at the apple.

"That's very bad luck," I said.

"How so?" Orestes asked. "What's the story? Tell us about it."

"It's my own story," I said. "Well, the part where Thetis and I got married."

"We're not budging till you tell us," Perdita said firmly.

"Before Zeus put us in charge of it," I started, "a visitor came to the Fold from Mount Ida in Anatolia, near where Troy once stood. The King of Troy, Priam, kept a royal herd of sheep up on the mountainside. Priam's son, Paris, was just a kid when Priam farmed him out to the Fold to learn the wool business from first ewe-drop. Paris was minding sheep when Zeus and Thetis were planning out our garden-party wedding. They had a long guest list, but they chose not to invite Eris, goddess of discord. As Zeus put it, 'Wherever she goes she takes trouble with her.'

"Undaunted, and true to her prickly nature, Eris showed up at the wedding anyway. She plopped this golden apple on the gift table with a card that read, 'For the Fairest.' Well, that led to a food fight involving Hera, Aphrodite, and Athena. To settle the matter, Zeus snatched Paris out of the Fold to choose the fairest. In a choice like that, there are no winners. The sheepish prince Paris settled nothing. He awarded the golden apple to Aphrodite. She rewarded Paris with Helen. Things went from a food fight to a ten-year war that ruined everything in that part of the world. You don't want to handle that apple. You sure don't want to start something like that again."

The kids backed away from the prop table. We picked up our gear and headed home. On the way back, they were not into swords, or apples, or flowers. They were entirely into each other. It was like I was just another prop on their private stage.

CHAPTER THREE

Orestes had a hard time leaving his sword back there, but I was firm about it. That was a month ago. Since then, he has been a good hand around the Fold. He's been real good with the dogs, but he'll never be comfortable with the sheep. He misses his hunting. He gets up in the night and just walks off in the moonlight, stalking. It's the closest he can come to his kind of hunting here.

Perdita has started making new clothes. If Orestes likes them, he says so, and she wears them. If he's not so keen, she tries something else. It's a subtle change in her. Thetis finds it disturbing.

"I didn't see this coming," she said the other day. "Am I losing it, Peleus? The foresight?"

"I don't think a goddess can lose it, Thetis," I said. "To me, the unexpected is more fun than it is for you. You've come to depend on your foresight. I like surprises more than you do."

"*Men*," she sniffed.

"Perdita seems fond of this one," I chuckled.

Thetis beamed. "I am thrilled. A mother frets about such things. I adore them both for the way they are adoring one another. I'm not so sanguine about how headstrong he is."

I said, "They come, and they go—the visitors to the Fold. I'm real happy that these have come."

"And if they go?"

"It will break my heart," I said.

"I do know. Oh my, I do know."

We were both shaken to the core by the next surprise. Perdita later told me how it came about.

In the hay loft, Orestes had another of those forebodings of his, a flash of something dreadful. He started to gasp for air. He threw his arms over his eyes. He couldn't breathe.

Perdita said, "What's wrong? Was it a dream?"

"No, I was awake. It came over me like before, remember? This time it was darker. This time I thought my father was dead, or about to die." Smiling, he murmured, "Are you all right?"

Perdita blushed and turned her head downward and away. "Yes, very. I love that you always ask. What did you just see?"

He said, "It's more what I felt, although I did see something. It was a bow and arrow. I was supposed to pick it up, but it was too heavy. I couldn't lift it. I knew I had to pull it up, but I knew if I did it would change everything—it would be the death of me."

Perdita lifted a pale straw and launched it over his head. "Orestes, we don't have bows and arrows or any of that stuff here. It's going to be all right. It was your imagination."

"It wasn't here. It was back at the palace, at my home. The bow and arrow: I know them. I've handled them easily before. They hang in the palace armory. They belong to my father, Agamemnon. But I have a dreadful feeling about him." Orestes absently massaged his forearm as if it were strained from an effort.

Perdita lolled back against the hay and threw handfuls of it upward. Two barn swallows flushed and swooped from a rafter out the open door. "Because he's at war?"

"Not exactly. He may be home from war. But he may be dead."

"Things are getting way too solemn for my liking," Perdita said. "You can't know that. It's your imagination. Let's take a long walk today, with a picnic."

"It wasn't imagination that stopped my breath just now. If he is dead, then I'm king of the Myceneans."

That sank into Perdita. Now it was her breath that became difficult. "What do you mean to do?"

Orestes said in a barely audible voice, "I have to know. I have to go back."

Perdita moaned, "Oh no."

"Come with me."

"I can't. I've never been beyond the Edge."

Orestes spoke in a rush, "Come to my palace. Be my wife. Be my queen."

Perdita's eyelids closed, "We can't just pick up and go. You're stuck here like the rest of us until your storyteller decides otherwise. That's my fate and that's yours."

"I don't know my storyteller, or even if there is such a thing. I'm the one who wants this."

Desperate now, Perdita urged, "Let's at least ask Thetis."

"Ask her what?"

"What you should do."

Orestes pondered a moment. "It's my choice. I don't need her for that. I'm in a hurry! What I need is to marry you. I love you, Perdita. Peleus will marry us, he's a king."

Perdita realized he had said this twice now. "Are you proposing to me?"

"Yes! Marry me, Perdita. Come away with me to begin a new life in a new land. Follow me as a wife must."

"Now I'm afraid. You said yourself that something dreadful might be happening where you're going."

Orestes stood and pulled her to her feet. "Yes, so we need to hurry. Come on. We'll talk to them this morning and head out when the sun is high."

THETIS AND I WERE in the kitchen when they returned. Dull bells clinked at the necks of sheep on the hillside behind the cottage.

Orestes came over to the open door, stood straight, and said solemnly, "King Peleus, we want to marry. Would you please perform the ritual?"

Thetis was distraught. Usually, I just go off to find a chore to do when she gets this way, but this time I stayed. I sensed a fight coming and the kids would be punching above their weight. Thetis moved into the open doorway, scowling at them. She pointed her long, spiny finger at Orestes. Her voice rent the air as she declared, "Take care in thoughts of departing. The skies look grimly and threaten present blusters!"

The hillside sheep made a din of clanks and bleats as they startled and loped away. Orestes stopped just inches from her outstretched finger, his breathing steady. He and Thetis glared at each other. Perdita quickened her step to his side. She gripped his hand. After a moment, Thetis smiled warmly, stepped aside, and gestured for them to enter with a motion that could stir an inland sea.

I looked at Thetis. Her face was impassive, her rose-petal eyes fixed somewhere beyond the cottage walls. I brought Orestes and Perdita tea and sheep's yogurt. I tried to make small talk, but they would have none of that. So, then I tried to explain that I was simply providing custodial care here at the Fold, tending to them for the sole purpose of returning them to their stories at the times picked by their storytellers. No one else could change their stories or their timelines. We all have to honor our stories by being faithful to our given purposes. It seemed so reasonable to me; I was patiently bringing them to drink at the well of sweet reason.

By this time Perdita was sitting next to Orestes and holding his hand. She had nodded in agreement with his statement and her jaw was set. She said, "Peleus, please don't deny me now, at the threshold of my happiness. When we get back from checking on Orestes' home, we'll build a small cottage near the Edge of the Fold. If you need extra help with the sheep, we'll be there. When Thetis goes off on one of her excursions to the sea, I'll come back and see to the kitchen and all the meals. It will all work out perfectly. It always does here at the Fold."

I said to them, "You aren't even listening to each other, let alone to me. Orestes doesn't want to just check on things, he has a premonition that would make him king of Mycenae, his domain. That's no small cottage on a sheep ranch. What then, Perdita? If you're married to him, then you'd be the queen of the storied House of Atreus. That's a heavy responsibility. We'd never see you back here again."

Perdita said nothing. She gave me a long look that seemed to say she needed to think about that some more.

I turned to Thetis. "I could use a little help, Thetis. I'm doing all the talking here."

She thundered, "I don't know what my sweet voice could add to your appeals, Peleus. You've laid the case correctly. I trust no one here expects me to sketch out a roadmap for what is yet to happen if you go this way or that way. I'm astonished that all your great minds and great thoughts have overlooked a detail I brought to your attention a month ago. Perdita is to be betrothed to the Prince of Bohemia."

Perdita made an agonized groan and gripped Orestes' hand harder.

Thetis chided, "Haven't you finished reading your play, child?"

Perdita pushed a strand of hair over her ear and said, "No I haven't. I've been busy with other things for the last month."

Orestes said, "Who's this Prince of Bohemia and why hasn't he been on the grounds for all this time that I've been here?"

Thetis said, quietly now, "You make a good point, he hasn't been here for months. His name is Florizel."

"Hah! Are you sure that's not the Queen of Bohemia's handmaiden? So, has he been off performing majestic labors as Heracles did? Or perhaps he's finished those and is leading an army to conquer new territory for this Bohemia he intends to govern."

"Now, now, no need to resort to sarcasm," Thetis said, with a twinkle in her eye. "He is laboring, but not under kingly tasks. He and his father labor under the misunderstanding that Perdita is a farm girl, not a highborn Sicilian."

"Perfect," said Orestes. "Let them continue to think it. We'll just head back to my domain where no one will mistake her as anyone less than *Queen!*"

Perdita spoke up. "Thetis, you know how I dislike uncertainty as much as you do. You can set our minds at rest. You know all the books and thus you know our stories. Tell Orestes now so we may be prepared for what lies ahead."

Orestes turned to Thetis, "You know how my story unfolds? By all means tell it to us now. It will make all the difference to us."

Thetis crossed her muscled legs, rustling her seafoam-gray housedress. She frowned and shook her head. "No, Orestes. Oh, I do know your story and how it ends. Since you have three story-tellers, you have three endings. But I'm not going to spoil your story for you. I made that mistake once.

"Achilles had two destinies. One was to die a hero for all times with a warrior's imperishable fame. The other was to live a long, fully realized life in the comfort of our little kingdom but in obscurity. I told him that he could choose either of these two destinies. His choice to die as a hero aborted my happiness.

"Zeus sent me to Troy to end his grief for the death of Patroclus. Instead, I witnessed his lurid sprint to his own young death. I watched light leave his eyes, even as his hair glowed an aura in the setting sun. I can still hear his last cry, not of anguish, but of wrath.

"My son's contagious grief infected my timeless life. I shall forever waken to see the Trojan prince's fetid arrow pierce that small spot of him I carelessly left unwashed! The vision spoils the start of every day and will do so for days without end. No, Orestes, I shan't be doing that again."

"I'm afraid," said Perdita.

"Well," Orestes began to reason, "You wouldn't have to reveal the ending, but you could watch over us and if we decide we're better off back here, you could bring us back."

"Oh, please!" Thetis scoffed. "I'm not going to bail you out whenever you whistle. You're so full of your own independence, exercise that free will of yours."

I didn't like where this was going. I whispered to Thetis, "But you won't just leave him there to die, will you? After what you went through with Achilles?"

Thetis clouded over. She can be mean when she's backed into a corner. But she grew very still. In a small, dry voice she whispered back, "No, I couldn't bear to watch this one die. You've found my own weak spot."

Her voice a soft quaver, she said, "Orestes, I just don't know whether you can come back here. I'm being frank with you. I'm no good when it comes to uncertainties that I can't foresee. Probably you would be stuck there, but maybe you could find a way to get back. It's never happened before. Look, dear, if you find yourself confronted with certain death, with nowhere else to turn, call for me. I'll do the best I can."

Thunder cracked and rolled slowly in echoes through the Fold. We all looked up—all, that is, but Thetis. She simply stood, walked out of the kitchen, and up the stairs. I could hear her start to sob. Then the rain hit in torrents.

Orestes said, "Let's get the ceremony over with. We have a long journey ahead."

Perdita hesitated. She said, "Well, can't it wait till tomorrow? Just look at that rain. Tomorrow should be better, right Peleus?"

I didn't look at her. I was studying Orestes. His mind was made up.

He said, "Perdita, I have to return, and I have to do it right now. I want Peleus to say the ritual and I want you to come with me as my wife."

Perdita was calm and radiant. She looked him in the eye and said, "We will marry, but not at the drop of a hat. You've only just proposed to me. I have an independent mind the same as you do. A wife has other responsibilities and there comes a time when she must be the prudent one. You go on your impetuous way, take care of your business, which I know nothing of, and then come back and become my husband. I'll be waiting for you."

"I may already be, and surely will become, a king. That's why I need you."

Perdita said, "You'll be back."

He shook his head slowly. "If you want me in your future, come with me. That's how it should be. A king needs an heir who shall become king, and on and on through the generations. I'll need you from the very start, not least for entertaining dignitaries. Unless you come now, I won't have you when I need you the most, and you will have no idea what's happening to me. It must be now, Perdita."

No one spoke. He turned and strode out the door into the rain and wind in the direction of the Edge. Perdita looked desperately at me. I had nothing to say. It was beyond me. She took hesitant steps to the door. Orestes was now out of sight.

She shrieked and ran toward the Edge. I grabbed my hat and coat and followed her. It was all I could do to keep up with her in the storm.

When we reached the Edge she shouted to him, "Wait!"

Orestes was at full stride heading down the center of the clover slope toward the scrim, which was now raised to head height. Blinding sunlight blazed ahead of him at the opening. Orestes stopped, his shoulders tensed, but he didn't turn around. Perdita came to his side. Both were drenched in alpine rain. Lightning flashed in the gloom. She sank to her knees.

"Stand, Perdita. Stand tall and walk with me to Mycenae."

"I'm trying to stand."

"You're not trying, you are frozen. I've seen deer freeze like that just before they die. Stand. Otherwise, you can't walk. You ran up to me just now, the least you can do is walk with me the rest of the way. Make your choice."

"We should stay. Is Mycenae more lush, more tranquil than here? We know what is here. You have no idea what may await you. Are you so greedy for a crown, Orestes? Do you walk away from perfection to wear a crown? I cannot. What you call 'an heir who shall become king' I call a baby. I want our babies, Orestes. Without you the only newborns I'll ever hold will have four legs. I ran to you just now to implore you to come to your senses and stay here where we know we have happiness. I'm so afraid."

"Perdita, it's up to you. Staying put is not an option for me."

"Not an option? Is this your 'destiny,' Orestes? I thought you wanted to choose your own way of life, not leave it up to some storyteller."

"I'm not even thinking about storytellers. It is more deep-rooted than that. All my life I have trained to answer the call, to march toward danger, not look for the easy way out. My honor is well understood in my homeland. I gain that honor by gaining the riches and the glory of a warrior king, just as all the kings I have ever known or heard of. It would be cowardice for me to stay behind in safety. That would *truly be greedy!* But I need you. I want you beside me, no one else."

She stammered through tears and rain. "It's better that you go on without me. You'll come back, Orestes. I'll have everything waiting for you and then we'll live in the Fold forever. We'll live quietly in a new cottage. We'll paint it white. We'll paint the trim purple, not black. We'll read the books Thetis has collected. It will be as if you never left."

Orestes tried to swallow but his mouth was too dry. He marched to the light spilling from beneath the scrim. He dug his foot into the soft, soaked turf, and stepped over the Edge.

CHAPTER FOUR

King Orestes though I may have become, I forgot my sword—*again!* It never occurred to me to take it off the prop table.

I stepped from the sheep-cropped clover of the Fold to the gritty, scorched beach on the southeast coast of Mycenae. You can't see our palace from here, but you can see this beach from the slope behind the palace. The palace compound sits on high ground between two mountains. From up there, Electra and I used to scan the coast and the horizon beyond it. I looked up in that direction, hoping to catch a glimpse of something, if only a curl of smoke from the kitchen. There was nothing. My feet burned, even in my sandals. I needed to run for cover.

I reached the marsh grass beside the salt-crusted bank of the brackish estuary. I was near the citadel on the outskirts of Tiryns. Cousin Pylades and I used to come here to watch the games at the Acropolis when his family visited from Phocis. Pylades was my best friend. We looked out for each other—we cared about each other in our hearts. He didn't carry the weight of the world on his shoulders as I did. We enjoyed kicking around questions. Mother was always too busy for that. Pylades kept things simple and grounded. He kept things in everyday perspective. I had gone to Phocis to live with him for a bit before reaching the Fold.

Many streams flow from the mountain slopes into the narrow end of the estuary. One branch rises from a spring, the Perseia, on the plateau where our palace sits. Long ago my ancestors built a cistern there to capture our household's needs for water before it spilled into its pathway to the sea. Pylades and I would hack trail marks on trees along the jumble of streambeds with our first, boy-sized *kopis*. Now, the marks were only faint, gray scars. Although at times our stream could be fat and angry, I found it to be barely a trickle now. *When there's time, I'll go to Phocis and have a visit with Pylades to catch up*, I thought. He'll want to know about the Fold. It reminds me of him—quiet, sensible, "everyday," as he likes to say.

It was a hard climb from the estuary. I paused briefly at the top of the stone stairway to our vast cisterns. To slake the thirst in the dank, cool cavity was always refreshing after the long climb. But when I reached it that day its air seemed dry with a putrid odor. I wanted to know why. But that task would have to wait until another day, after I learned the fate of my father.

He and the other kings had set out to restore Aunt Helen to her rightful husband. They were duty-bound to do so under sworn oath pledged to Tyndareus at Helen's wedding. Agamemnon was commanding general of the combined armies of the Greek kingdoms that assaulted Troy for the crime of Paris who abducted her. King Peleus had not taken the oath to protect Helen. Peleus chose a path of peace and look where it landed him: the Fold is a paradise. What he lacks are the trappings of success and honor. He found enviable tranquility in his chosen life—so different from the lessons handed down to me by my own father. I wondered whether Perdita and I would ever live in such tranquility together.

I reached the oval wall of the compound at late dusk just as the moon appeared in the notch of mountains beyond our plateau. The wall encloses the palace, several other households, and a burial ground inside the Lion Gate, all made from stacked mountain stone. I had thought to enter by the second, smaller gate at the rear, but I was attracted to a clamor going on inside the main one. I knew the drumbeat. The off-count pattern was Electra's dance. I heard three voices chanting: Electra and Chrysothemis, my sisters, and…who is that one? Pylades? Yes! *Good luck, this*, I thought.

I hid beside the gate, now just a windy cavity, its timbered door long since burned in winter. I could easily see the weedy stretch of street and ancient burial plots. Most of the wooden roofs had collapsed. Trembling rodents hunted at the broken doorway of the granary. Nowhere scurried a fat, irritated hen. The air bore no scent of the thick red wine of late summer birthday teasing. Apparent to the senses was no trace of human commonplace. All that remained were unoccupied rocks and bare, unguarded, ungated enclosure.

Then, I saw Pylades kiss Electra. *Well, well.*

The three of them began to dance staccato steps to Electra's drum, pausing only to chant, open-armed, to the rising full moon:

CHRYSOTHEMIS: *Artemis, moon-crowned goddess of the hunt and womb, your father, Zeus, made you a lion among women, with leave to kill any wild beast for pleasure.*

PYLADES: *Over windy peaks you draw your golden bow, rejoicing in the chase, and send out grievous shafts. Mountains tremble with the feral cries of dying boar, hawk, and hare. You, with cold heart, destroy entire races of them.*

ELECTRA: *King Agamemnon's arrow killed but one stag, your beloved pet. By whose charter gained you the power to claim the life of my innocent sister in trade?*

CHRYSOTHEMIS: *Your fury would not slake until he paid a debt of grief for his mistake. Your heart could not be cheered until you ransomed father's child, my sister, for fair winds to move his warships.*

ELECTRA: *You, who becalmed the entire fleet, could not calm your thirst for blood without the sacrifice of Agamemnon's virgin daughter. His loss of love so filled your heart with joy you filled the sails of a thousand ships bound for ten years of bloodshed. One virgin for one stag, and into the bargain the deaths of Troy and countless men of Greece!*

They could only mean beloved Iphigenia! I started toward them but stopped as they resumed their chorale:

ELECTRA: *This circular grave…*

PYLADES: *The bitch Queen had it dug…*

CHRYSOTHEMIS: *…down as a shaft, "to take less space,"*

PYLADES: *…said the Queen, the bitch!*

ELECTRA: *Thus, my pale father stands like a post in its hole,*

PYLADES: *Stands under the air,*

ELECTRA: *Yet not in the underworld,*

CHRYSOTHEMIS: *For she, the bitch, refused a warrior his funeral pyre.*

ELECTRA: *Agamemnon stands unnoticed like broken pots beneath a midden heap.*

"*No!*" I shouted, my head thrown back, my throat on fire. "No, it cannot be so. Agamemnon, commander of all the Greeks! Father! The heartbeat of this palace! It cannot be!"

Electra turned to face me, and her eyes went wild. She triple-time-stamped her feet like a crazed puppy. In her high-pitched, parched voice, "Is that you? You can't be! Who?"

She looked so much older. Her narrow face was gaunt and unpretty from neglect and she had bruising at each cheekbone. Her legs were bony and scabbed. Pylades wrapped his arms around Electra and drew her close as they gaped at me.

Chrysothemis spoke first, "Glad you could find your way, Orestes. Most would have forgotten it after ten years."

Electra wrested free and ran to me. She stared. She touched my head. "It is you; it is your hair. Sister, do not speak sharply to the brother we have prayed for. Here is our answered prayer. Here is our plan at last. Here is our revenge." Her hands trembled. Only with exertion could she grip with the strength I remembered. She no longer resembled a palace flower; now she quaked like a forest creature in a snare.

I said, "Revenge, Electra? Revenge for our sister is for the professionals. The immortal Furies exact revenge as their exclusive specialty. Have you not summoned them?"

Electra shook herself from my arms. She shuddered, saying, "Oh, Orestes, you have been away too long. Iphigenia was ten slow years ago. Revenge for her would be stale at this point..."

I interrupted, "Revenge never grows stale! Revenge never expires, ever!"

She continued, "A good sentiment, well said. But I mean there is fresh kill to avenge, Orestes. Why do you think your father stands sentinel, unseeing, beneath the ground we stand on? Why here, not the Trojan sand dunes? Why did he die in Mycenae after conquering Troy?"

I was bewildered. It could not have been ten years that I had been gone. It seemed perhaps ten months since I last saw my sister and this palace. But my eyes told me that, indeed, at least ten years had taken their toll on both. "I cannot answer that, Electra. I have not seen war and decay. I have seen tranquility, and it suits me. Explain the inexplicable death of King Agamemnon. No one outside Troy would have either cause or skill to take his life, certainly not in his own home."

Electra said, "I sent you away in hopes you would find respite from the horrors of home. I'm glad I succeeded. But now you have returned. Perhaps you have observed that our homeland is slightly less than tranquil at this point. It is not the Trojan army that fouled our nest. It was internal corruption and madness within our family circle, brother dear."

She relaxed her face into a wry smile. "Tranquility suits you, Orestes. Mourning suits me better. Mourning is my black bridal veil, more to be borne than worn. I did not choose it, it chose me. I married grief."

I reached for her hand, "Electra, I have a choice."

She sighed. "And in choosing tranquility you gain only naiveté."

"If you have no choice," I said, "You have no life."

She nodded slowly, "There, that says it all. Now you, too, have no choice in Mycenae. You have a foretold errand at home. Listen to me. You are right, skill alone could not defeat our father. It happened through deception and entrapment. As for cause, it was the oldest: the lust for power. As for whose lust, well, Queen Clytemnestra is the expert on that. She and usurper Aegisthus. Clytemnestra sought revenge for the sacrifice of Iphigenia that Agamemnon had commanded. Cousin Aegisthus just loves watching us stew as he savors the monarchy.

"But even Agamemnon had resorted to deception and trick. He had sent for mother and sister to join him at the port of embarkation. He promised them that Iphigenia would marry swift-footed Achilles before the invasion. When they arrived for rapturous nuptials, the soothsayers dragged our sister to the sacrificial stone, drew a knife across her still-unkissed throat, and stole her life to appease that bloodless, rising moon! Then, he went away on his own bloodthirsty business and stayed away ten years while his home and family crumbled to what you see around you.

"And so, when the signal fires told of Troy's fall, Mother and Aegisthus began preparations for Father's return. All bowing and scraping in smarmy adulation, they welcomed Agamemnon with his war-prize girlfriend, Cassandra. Aegisthus conspired with our mother. With their very own hands they axe-slaughtered both hero and prize. Now, if their conspiratorial regicide and defiling of your father's corpse are not enough to get your blood boiling, Orestes, I don't know what will!"

I was stunned. What did she expect me to do? "The Furies, Electra. That's who we need for this."

I could smell Electra's outrage. "You want Furies, Orestes? You'll never get them! Listen to me. It is just us, not the gods and not the soldiers. Your mother swallows honeyed wine in your father's bed till she vomits. Not only did this hateful cousin co-execute our father, he spends your dwindling treasury and gets his jollies by smacking the maids and me around. We have intolerable pain and loss. You are here for a reason, Orestes. You are our hope. Rid us of the poisonous Aegisthus and drain the sour, murderous blood of drink-wasted Clytemnestra. The Furies haven't lifted a hand to help us in the ten years since Iphigenia was murdered. They didn't appear when Clytemnestra hacked your father to death. Why would you expect them now? Who else but you do you expect will avenge the evils I've just told you of? And don't overlook the silver lining here: we are so much yesterday's rubbish that the Furies don't care what you do. We seem unworthy of even them. Do this without worry of the Furies descending on you."

Pylades spoke up quickly. "Electra don't say that. You know nothing of the gods, especially those of the underworld. The Furies are nothing to trifle with. They may be tardy but must never be forgotten. Orestes, if you decide to follow Electra's plea for revenge, be assured the Furies will know and will pursue you unrelentingly for their own revenge. Be prepared with a backup plan for that. It is not some possible eventuality, it is a certainty—a dead certainty. Matricide will bring them, even though the rest of this mess did not."

The three of them grew subdued. They had wept and chanted and danced their ten-year pain and were exhausted. Whether for ten months or ten years, I was out of time and out of touch. I had experienced more tranquility, beauty, meditation on life in, let's call it ten months, than these dear creatures had in ten years. I knew where they belonged, and it wasn't in this rubble of grotesque memories. They needed to live on a certain sheep farm fresh in my memory, where the cottages are black-trimmed-pastel, happy homes of laughter with sublime hay lofts. *Might I be able to take them there? Thetis didn't say I could return, nor did she completely rule it out.*

I looked at the hollow, darkened shapes of what had been the royal city. *Are they doomed to remain in this barren place? Am I? I do believe I have the will to choose. I do believe I have the right to live according to good choices. I believe my dear sisters and friend do too. I must find a way.*

Chrysothemis said, "You seem preoccupied, Orestes. Perhaps our small worries are not enough to hold your attention. Electra has proposed a task. It is way simpler than, for example, the lightest labors of Heracles. You are a man, are you not? You have at least gained the years of one. Are you muddling over how you should do this task or whether to? May we bring you something to stir your courage? Or do you await instruction from a master? We all have masters, Orestes, don't kid yourself."

My princess sister, gold of the earth, and I never were of the same mind the way I was with Electra. I might make progress discussing ideas of freedom and independence with Electra, but I feared it would be fruitless with Chrysothemis. Her words nettled me, but then, she had every reason to be bitter and cynical. Just because she did, I did not need to be.

"I'm torn, Chryssy. The ordeals you have experienced deserve vengeful action. Iphigenia and Father deserve it. The corruption ruling his house and dynasty must end. But I am a hunter of game, not men and women. I trained, of course. But I do not live to take human life. I value the potential in my life and that of everyone else. Although I never went to war against Trojans, I warred against wild game, stags, and boar. I was alone for weeks at a time. Every bird in the pot would get me through the next day of hunting. In the north, where timber forests grow as thick as laurels do here, my prey were larger and more wily. I devoted all my energy and skill to hunting them. Their numbers in my bags measured my wealth. I know how each of them died. And still I killed. As for Clytemnestra, she may deserve to die, but I do not deserve to be the one to execute her."

"Saying it that way," she answered, "Gives her impunity. There is no one else but you. It is expected of you, by family and gods alike. Our royal family line ends with you. Your legacy and your destiny require you to clean the House of Atreus, marry Hermione as was promised years ago, and create a succession to the throne."

I thought of Perdita and the Bohemian evening rains. "It would not be the same on this barren, forgotten rock." I muttered. Pylades heard me.

He said, softly, "The same as what, Orestes? We should listen to you now and pause our talk of matricide. Electra said our woes are insufficient to boil your manly blood. Then tell us what does. The night is long and holds moonlight till dawn. We've told you of our tormented ten years. We should listen to what your mind values more than duty to your legacy in the home of your birth. Convince us, if you can, what outweighs restoring your rightful monarchy with Helen's daughter as your queen to mother enough heirs to fill future epics. Tell us why we should follow you to dark forests far from the land of our birth, even if we could."

Curiosity over that seemed to get the better of Electra. She breathed deeply and, for the first time, sat. She gathered a knitted shawl around her frail body and looked dolefully at me.

"You have his challenge. Let's see what you've got."

Chrysothemis spread a deerskin beside her sister and sat, unable to hide a smirk. Pylades stayed at my side. He smiled. "This is better. Tell us your adventures and discoveries."

CHAPTER FIVE

Nearby was a building stone that had fallen from the city wall. I didn't want to tower over them, my closest thing to a family, so I sat on the stone and bent forward. Pylades sank to his knees and then shifted over to half-recline, propped on one arm.

"Electra, you sent me away," I began, "Because you feared Aegisthus would see me as an obstacle to his ambition. I understood your fears, but I did not run because of danger. I simply removed the treasure he should not be able to plunder: my rightful claim to Mycenae's throne. Every day brought new sights and sounds. I lived from campfire to campfire, foraging and hunting. I reveled in the hunt. Although Artemis may have taken our Iphigenia, she instilled in me the need and skill to hunt. Hunting became a voracious pursuit for me. I began to realize that I could thrive using just my own skills put to this purpose. I did not need the generosity of strangers, though I often received it. I did not need the officers of Mycenean training camps. I especially did not need the schooling of a sinister mother or even our loving nurse, Cilissa. I did not need favors from Olympian gods for sanctuary. This understanding fed my mind as much as the game that kept me alive for day after day of trekking and hunting. I welcomed the certainty and comfort of that knowledge. I felt that I was enough—competent to live a self-sufficient life and worthy of happiness.

"But where in the world was I going? Not in the sense of what *polis* was next down the road, but in the sense of some purpose besides hunting. I could only think of it vaguely, something like living a good life, whatever that is.

"I reached forested mountains after leaving Phocis. The people did not speak our language or anything like it. 'Barbarians,' as our teachers told us, but they didn't know that. They were strong and happy. They were proud of their lives, their music, and their languages. But they were vulnerable, living apart from others. I could see their need to be unified without destroying their uniqueness.

"Then there came a day that ended before I had prepared myself for night. It was past time to hunt but still I left the road and began stalking. Night fell. I crawled. I became ensnared in some sort of mesh. I thrust my sword forward and tore the mesh. I walked through the ripped fabric, and into a new land."

"You mean you had eaten too many barbarian mushrooms," Chrysothemis interjected.

Electra smiled for the first time that night. Pylades shot them a frown. My back ached. I needed to sum things up.

"It was foreign in every way, a sheep ranch, but unlike any you've seen. The shepherds tended to more than sheep. I met a girl."

"It took you long enough to get to that part," Chrysothemis spat. "All this la-di-da philosophy boils down to something a lot more basic than self-discovery."

Electra shoved her elbow into Chryssy's ribs and said, "Well, Orestes, can we skip over the salacious part and just get to the part where you actually answer Pylades's original question?"

"Electra, that was the answer. Maybe it is not as salacious, or even majestic, as you have in mind, but for me it is enough."

Electra shook her head and said, "Not on your life, Orestes, you're already spoken for. You are engaged to Cousin Hermione. That was the will of Grandfather Tyndareus, and that's that. You have no choice in the matter of marriage. You are the last heir to the throne of *this realm*, not some misty vale of bliss. We need you right here to be fecund in matters dynastic. More immediately, your purpose is simple vengeance.

"Spare me the temptations to run away with you! My fate is sealed here. I'm clear-eyed about the matter of choices: I have none, zero! The same goes for Pylades and Chryssy. We know our duty and we know yours. The ancient, good people of our ancestral land are poor and bereft of hope. They need a king. They need you. As things are now, they have a pair of criminal autocrats on the thrones of Atreus. Don't you care about them? Is this farmer's daughter of yours such a siren that you would abandon everyone in your history just to wimp yourself on love-wobbled knees to wherever she has a notion to beckon you? Your blood kin and heritage rot before your eyes and all you can do is swoon and swan in thrall to a distant milkmaid?"

I protested, "I want what's best for the four of us standing here, and it is definitely not to remain standing here! I know what will instill life and purpose to your souls: it is the freedom and the will to live by genuine choices. I can take you to a beautiful green land where you would enjoy that freedom. I'm sick and tired of living by some fateful destiny, or some story told by an unseen bard. I am not a man of war. I cannot conquer new lands or scoop up glittering loot from a defeated people."

Pylades said, "Look here friend, the life you describe is not the luxury of kings. Kings have commitments and duties, whether in war or peace. Your father's war with Troy may be over, but your war is here and now, on this rocky, wasted hilltop. What does it matter that it is no longer green and lush? It could be. It should be. Where is your vision, man?"

I said, "My vision is for quiet days, fair issue, and a long life. My vision of a good life has no room for war."

"No war?" scoffed Chrysothemis. "No killing? Where did you get that notion? War was your father's craft, and his father's, and all the generations of the men of Mycenae from time out of mind. Mycenae now lies in ruins. Your treasury is bone dry, and there is nothing left to sell. How do you expect to get our ancestral home up and running again? You do it the old-fashioned way, Orestes: you plunder. Troy may be out of the picture but there are plenty of other places. There's been talk of making a run at Sicily, but that'd be a reach. The Persians are to be reckoned with as well. You think Troy was a city of gold? Troy was an outback trading post compared to the cities to the south of it. You're going to be on the march, sleeping under the stars. contemplating death, and pillaging the rest of your life. You're only twenty-six now, so I'd say you have a whole lot of killing ahead of you. You'll be fine; the first time's the hardest.

"War is never over. Your dream of peace and quiet, a houseful of kids, and old age can only happen in your dreams. What good are dreams like that when you are facing a thousand barbarian chariots of sweaty fanatics coming after your wife and daughters? Your hand must always hold the sword. Um. Where *is* your sword, Orestes?"

"Never mind that."

Electra clutched the shawl closer in fists drawn under her chin. She sighed and said, "I understand you want to be the independent thinker, so put on your thinking cap. Find an answer before dawn that suits both your free will and our family's vengeance. I'm taking a nap. Forget your farm girl fling and behave like the King of Mycenae which you now are. Find a way to want what I want. Find it in action right here, your home, your birthright, and your destiny—here, not on greener pastures somewhere else."

That ended the entire discussion. Pylades shrugged sympathetically and he, too, stretched out beside Electra to sleep. They looked all the ten years they'd endured since I last saw them, and they looked right together. I'd never thought of them that way before but now I could picture them as a married couple raising a family. If anyone could get Electra healthy again it would be Pylades. It was a comfort to me. He would be just what this family needed. I was too hungry and stimulated now for sleep. My mind turned and fretted.

But what about me? Could I fit in here? Even if I could is that what I want? Looking at my sister with my best friend set off a yearning for the happiness Perdita and I had come to know. *So, which do I want more: the Mycenean throne or a cottage on a remote sheep ranch? The real question is: Perdita or Hermione? As to that, there is no doubt. It must be Perdita, no matter what the place might be or my place in it.*

With Father dead, the responsibility of the House of Atreus fell on me; that much was preordained. Also ordained was the political choice by my parents to marry Hermione, whom I hadn't seen in nearly twenty years, when we were just kids. She probably didn't like the idea any more than I did, and probably less so now. Not much happiness in that picture!

The moon was setting when Pylades came next to me. "You should hide yourself. People are stirring."

People appeared on the broken street as a slow-moving clutch of a half-dozen haggard servant women from the palace. Pylades draped Electra's shawl and the deerskin around my shoulders. He said, "That purple trim on your tunic gives you away, Orestes. Pretend you are a beggar from another land, and you won't be noticed. Stand over here with me, behind this column, we'll just listen in."

The women were hollow-eyed and moved in what I can only describe as a stumble. They each carried a pitcher or an urn of something. They gathered around the shaft-shaped grave of my father and began lamentations.

The first woman was bent with age and labors. She poured a measure of the water from her clay pitcher and sprinkled it on the dusty grave top as if she had just seeded it in springtime.

"King Agamemnon," she wailed, "your queen-wife-butcher bids me quench your dry throat with this water that is desperately needed in the palace kitchen, so scarce now that the cistern is polluted. In vain I pour your libation since your agonized throat was hacked by your mate and her lover, your cousin. So, take these tantalizing drops. It will not ease your pain, but it will staunch for a while the guilt stuck in the throat that drinks your vintage wine. Clytemnestra sent me with her apologies for not coming. She would have brought it herself were she not sleeping off a senseless stupor."

I turned to Pylades and said, "I know her! She is my old nurse, Cilissa."

"Shhhh," he whispered, "Yes she is. Take a good look at her in the fading moonlight."

I recoiled. "She is wretched."

Pylades shrugged, "She is an Atreus house leftover."

The remaining women resignedly waited their turns before pouring more precious water and wine and scented oils over the grave circle.

One of them glanced our way. "Who's there?"

Pylades muttered, "Two travelers. We come from Phocis. We would welcome a quiet bed and something to eat."

At that the woman bent over with a laugh that sounded like crushed seashells.

"Would you now," spat Cilissa. "Well then, if the truth be known, the servants of this palace, whose lives have diminished each day for ten years, would welcome that as well!"

"Phocis, you say?" asked one of the women. "Let's have a look at you. I remember kin of the master who would bring us gifts from Phocis on their visits. Those days are lost to a black history."

I ventured to ask a question that had troubled me. I turned my head away, under the shawl, and said, "The houses of this street leading to the palace: where are their owners? Their families?"

A slender woman with a long face and thatched hair said, "Who knows? Over ten years, those who didn't die simply moved on. Would you be looking to buy a fixer-upper? It's a good time to be in the market. Mind you, the taxes will kill you." She tilted her head back and howled through tears.

The women moved off again, back to the palace. I thought, *the future for me here is bleak. The prospect of returning to the Fold is even bleaker.* My head hurt. Sitting on stone grew tiresome. I slipped to the dusty ground and decided to rest my eyes.

Then it came to me, just as sunrise flooded the burial grounds of my family.

CHAPTER SIX

"Electra wake up! We have assassinations to conduct. I'll need breakfast after. Right now, I need Father's bow. Kindly sneak it out of the armory for me. Where is Chryssy?"

"She and Pylades went back to the palace at first light. My, aren't you up and at 'em early," she said with a grin. "I guess all you needed was some sleep."

"Come on, Electra, enough about mood swings, I need that bow."

"You're standing on it."

That stopped me. I looked at her expecting laughter. She was serious.

"It's buried with Agamemnon: not as grave goods, it was just to keep him propped up while they filled in the hole. I'll run to the granary to get you a shovel."

Dull details, I thought. *Great and dangerous thoughts come down to the dull details. I've prepared my conscience for mother-murder, but first I have to dig up the weapon.*

She returned, dragging the simple shovel. Her muscles were so wasted. I ached to gather her in my arms and carry her to the Fold for sheep's yogurt and biscuits and those books. She would adore the books. *Can't think about that now. There's wet business ahead. So hungry!*

The burial ground was tamped hard after the unceremonious burial of my father. This would be difficult. Nothing's easy. But it was my one and only chance to regain Perdita and choose my own way of life.

Clunk. The shovel struck something—well, it could only be one thing. *Too shallow! It's not right.* With tender care, this time with my hands, I uncovered the tip of the bow, just at the nape of Agamemnon's neck. The sun went higher, as did the smell of assassination. I was terrified. Handful by handful, I loosened, scooped, and scooped. I could push the bow now a little to the side. I rotated it and it loosened more. I stood astride the pitiful grave, gripped the bow, and lifted. But it didn't budge. Electra knelt to try scooping more granular rock dust. I watched her frustration grow.

"Electra, that's enough. It's up to me now. Give me space." She moved away. Again, I straddled the grave. I bent my knees, gripped the half-exposed bow, and tensed my legs. I felt the thing move. Three deep breaths, squat again, tense, strain, lift. Oh! It seemed to be rooted, but it moved—all of it. I staggered back, holding it in sore hands. Electra uttered a childish sound and clapped her hands.

"Now comes the hard part, Electra."

"MOTHER, THERE'S SOMEONE HERE to see you, put something on," Electra said, in a singsong.

I stood at the corner of my mother's bedroom doorway, peeking in at the edge of the tattered fabric that served as a door.

Gone were the tiled, mosaic panoramas of olive harvests and sheaves of grain that once adorned the king's hallway walls. A servant girl staggered under the weight of a copper commode she carried from Aegisthus's bedroom. She limped past me. She did not even see me. She held her battered face away from the pot in disgust over her errand. I recoiled at the sound of the usurper's belch from the room she had just left. I turned to listen again at the door.

Electra stepped around the clutter of gold cups scattered on the stone floor and pulled back the ancient woolen draperies covering the west wall window.

"Who is it? And close the drapes. My eyes hurt."

"A surprise!"

"I'm not dressed for surprises. And besides, unexpected guests are unwelcome in the palace these days. They lead to all that hemorrhaging."

"Mother don't be so negative. This surprise is not new. He's twenty-six and he's family."

Clytemnestra sat up straight. She clutched her hair and attempted to rake the tangles with her nails. "Don't prank me, Electra. That almost sounds like Orestes."

Electra spun on her malnourished legs with her arms outstretched. "Exactly right Mother! He just showed up on our doorstep. He has a lot to say. Shall I organize a welcome feast?"

Clytemnestra processed Electra's words and slumped against a damp pillow. Her face was unhappy. "This isn't a good time for company, dear."

"No company? Very well, no feasting. But surely I can bring him to see you. He's anxious to greet you."

"I doubt that," Clytemnestra slurred. "I'd be more comfortable seeing him with a couple of palace guards beside me."

Electra laughed gaily. "Such a tease. Come on now, have some water and comb your hair. He's waiting just outside your door."

"Why is he here now after all this time?" she whined. "Did you send for him? Naughty girl."

As Clytemnestra nattered, Electra stepped to the bedroom doorway and drew open the fabric door. Clytemnestra sat up again and swung her swollen legs over the edge of the bed. I stepped into the opening. In her chambers I saw my fate.

I gagged in revulsion at the sight of her. It brought back the memory of the sun-roasted stench of the circular grave this woman threw my father into like spoiled meat. She was the debauched criminal who turned my nurse into a malnourished whimperer. She was the mother who for ten years denied my sisters the essentials of life itself, never mind life's comforts. She was the wife who, in the slippery slosh of royal blood and entrails of her husband, cleaved nakedly to his triumphant first cousin. This was not a queen. This was not the mother I loved as a boy. She was unworthy of breath.

"Things still need sorting out," Clytemnestra continued. "The place is filthy. There is no time to put things right. His old room has rats. I'm uneasy having him here all of a sudden. No, I'm actually fearful. Look, Electra, you go to him and tell him to—"

The arrow struck her chest with such force that her over-fed, now lifeless, body tumbled backward, bloated legs thrashing. Electra let out a scream—one of surprise more than horror. Her scream drew attention; I heard footsteps. I turned back to see Aegisthus looking out from his bedroom at the corner of the long hall where I stood.

Pylades shouted from around the corner, down the other hall-way. "She's not receiving visitors, Sire," he said.

Aegisthus blinked and started to turn toward the sound. I nocked another arrow, raised my bow, drew the sinew, exhaled, and released. Aegisthus gurgled to silence when the arrow pierced the roof of his mouth and pinned the crown of his head against the corner wall. I was panting when Electra ran to hold my throbbing forearm.

She said warmly, "Now, let's get you some breakfast."

"I'm not hungry."

CHAPTER SEVEN

"What changed your mind last night, Orestes?" Pylades asked. He was rubbing salve on my sore forearm where the bowstring had sliced the skin.

"I've decided I can't stay here, Pylades; it's like a prison. My past is here, my crime is here, but not my future. Certainly not the future Chryssy painted for me. Electra asked what makes my blood boil. It is this: separation from the woman I love; separation from the place I love. That's what heats the blood, but it boils when the separation is imposed by someone, or something, else. I absolutely must return to that place, the place where I'll marry Perdita, the girl I told you about. Electra insisted on revenge, and she prompted me to think how to satisfy all of us in a single plan. It came to me this morning.

"I can return to the Fold with the help of Thetis, who runs that place with Peleus. Thetis will only come to help me if I am in mortal danger. So, I had to put myself in mortal danger. You said yourself that if I killed Clytemnestra the Furies would pursue me to avenge her death. My only chance for a future with Perdita is to expose myself to the wrath of the Furies and then call on Thetis for help."

"You've abandoned all caution, Orestes, and likely all common sense," Pylades said. The Furies will come. You have to flee."

"I'll stand my ground here," I said. "What better place?"

"That beach you were on yesterday. Thetis swims. How do you expect her to get up here?"

Pylades made perfect sense; he always did.

Just then he brought both his hands from my forearm to cover his ears and closed his eyes. The floor trembled.

"What's wrong?" I said. Then I heard it, a high-pitched shriek like an eagle, but not from the sky. It came from underground in a bubble of black ooze at the Lion Gate. Black smoke erupted from the ooze and parted into a three-headed, writhing viper shaped in smoke. Now three scratchy voices hissed in rage. Pylades fell to the floor in agony from the sound.

A cry of "Flee!" came from deep in his throat. Judging from the supernatural rocking of the ground, the piercing wails, the three ghastly figures swirling toward our courtyard, it made per-fect sense.

"We are the Erinyes, the Furies," came three screeches in unison. *"We are fate, we are fortune, and we can be a lady, a mother, a goddess, a you-name-it. For you, today, we'll be the triplet spawn of a fired-up, oversized Aesculapian tree adder!"*

"Hear me, Orestes, hear the name Alecto. You will know the inti-mate embrace of my rapacious anger. You have earned it, dear Orestes. Your deplorable ancestors cannibalized each other's heirs. That may have sickened me, but you have finally pissed me off!"

I looked into Electra's frightened eyes. "Now I am truly alone," she said. I picked up a gold goblet and lobbed it to Pylades.

"Take this and find the rest of the place settings. I want you to have whatever you find. As your last pledge, please look after my sisters. Electra, don't be alone. Marry Pylades. He will make a better husband than grief. Build a proper tomb for our father, one that will last."

Pylades then lobbed to me his *xiphos*. It made a half-turn in its arc, and I caught its handle. I nodded to him in respect and gratitude.

Electra said, "Take the sword and outrace the Furies to Delphi. There, you must plead with Apollo to rescue you. There, too, you must use Pylades' sword to slay Hermione's new husband!"

"*Who?*"

"Neoptolemus."

"*I've never heard of him!*"

"Just do it! He is the son of Achilles, but never mind that, it doesn't matter. He has your promised queen. You'll have to dispose of him to get her back. You've killed twice already today, the next one should be easy."

"*Nooooo!*" I roared. "You never mentioned him before. I've already lopped two limbs off this accursed family tree. Chryssy was right. The killing never stops in this family!'

Three hideous, sore-throated howls of laughter erupted from the parched earth. "*Pay attention to your underfed sister, Orestes. We're off to the races with you! She's got it down pat, and you're just coming of age in the storied Bronze Age.*"

Electra tightened her lips and motioned me to go with a jerk of her head. I ran. I ran like the squealing, husk-toothed boar I once hunted, less from free will than in abject terror. The sounds grew.

"*Hear me, Orestes, hear the name Megaera. I am the jealous one, sweetie pie. I'm not jealous of your sheepish romps in Bohemia, dear philosophical man, nor of your cringeworthy affection for weepy, over-dreary Electra. I am jealous only of my sisters, should either of them gnash your windpipe in her voracious maw before I swallow your soul. Such is the victory drink of a Fury's justice."*

I stumbled down along the shallow creek, frightful hours of flailing through underbrush and fallen branches, intent only on reaching the beach. In pursuit, the Furies swallowed whole shrubs, birds, rabbits—anything and everything in their path. As they puffed and tumbled, they grew in size as if every gasp and swallow inflated their smokey, scaly torsos and shuddering heads. The shadows of their bloated shapes behind me darkened the twisted path to the estuary.

"Don't fall for my sisters' endearing words, vile honeybun! Wait for me, Tisiphone! I'm the one who avenges murder, and you rang my bell today with your walk-off triple: king, queen, mother—bing, bang, boom! Oh, but Orestes, that's not all you are—you lousy matricider—you dare to deny fate! Not just tempt fate, as with this foolhardy stunt to tempt us into combat. You and that 'free will' of yours have denied fate as a simple fact of life. You profess to be the enemy of fate and what has it got you? You won the whole shebang: the eternal enmity of three immortal executioners! You cannot run or hide from the curse now etched in your bowels, the curse of revenge and untimely death. This heavy curse is exquisitely inescapable."

Then Megaera became Tisiphone's scaly boa, encircling her sister's neck, inducing a volcanic whoosh, followed by a lewd kiss. *"My one-third sister, now at a loss for words, has it only half right,"* hissed the constricting sister. *"We mean that you trespassed into our patch today! We avenge as an exclusive guild. Usurper your corrupted cousin may have been, and evil may have been your mum, but you crossed the usurper-line yourself when you crossed them off our bucket list! We'd have gotten to them, impatient body-poacher, in our own capricious time. You may not acquire time; time is as it may be given or refused you. I speak, you listen, your time is short. It's time we had you for breakfast, over easy, with center-cut bacon and grits."*

I could not escape the hair-frizzing dissonance of their oily snake-voices. I was back on the hot sand facing churning breakers of the incoming tide. I turned and ran to the edge of the cove and climbed flint-ribbed rocks to better scan the sea.

Tisiphone hacked hoarsely, *"Now you've done it, you insignificant little pissant! To gain a lookout rock you have lost ground on which to run."*

The reptile-vixens surrounded me. They coughed black clouds that stung my eyes. Back arched, elbows out, with hands at her shallow breasts, Alecto sang in diva falsetto,

"For whom do you squint?
Whom can't you see?
Ship not coming in?
Désole, mon chéri! It
Matters not to me!"

It was time. It was now or never. I was hemmed in by rock and sea. The Furies were right, I had run myself into the blind end of a maze. I cupped my hands to my mouth, turned seaward, inhaled, and screamed for Thetis. Twice. But before I could utter her name a third time, Megaera's sooty mouth covered my cupped hands, and she coughed contagion from her lungs into mine. I gagged, scorched from its corrosion. Worse, I was made mute—a setback in the Thetis plan.

But I could still fight. As trained, I concentrated on them one at a time. *I am a warrior king of Argos, and one of us is equal to a battalion of barbarians!* I thought of Perdita, my princess who should be my queen. This tripartite reptilian fate buzzing me from all directions blocked my future happiness with her. The excruciating terror that my existence might end without holding her again fueled my strength. I gripped the handle and whirled Pylades' sword, stabbing and hacking. Finally, my sword tip found a point of weakness. My repeated jabs infuriated the crazed, neck-winding dragon ladies even more. I couldn't breathe. My vision tunneled. Then, my legs went limp.

The wind shifted. It circled ever faster into a vortex. Salty fog replaced the black acidic clouds. The roar of a mighty wave drowned out the rude taunts of the furious creatures. A corrective third wave moved toward my rocky ledge, bearing a dolphin breaching at its curl. Atop the dolphin stood the doughty, four-foot-nine Thetis. Above her head, her outstretched right fist swirled and swept an astonishingly long strand of brown-green seaweed, hissing corkscrew curls of spray—a Sargasso lasso. Its whipping loop flung the snake-scaled dragon fliers into the ocean, so alien to an earth goddess. Steam erupted from the splash, roasting in midair errant gulls caught in the updraft.

CHAPTER EIGHT

Zeus had said to me at our wedding, "Peleus, you've a generous spirit to take this step. Get used to the prospect of her disappearing for days at a time. She won't be unfaithful on these forays. As a Nereid she is a reservist coast guardsman, always on call to rescue mariners thrown overboard in storms at sea. Since she is only one of fifty, and with ship traffic on the uptick, it'll happen when you least expect it."

So, I wasn't surprised to find her gone one late winter morning. Before that, she and I had decided to try to cheer up Perdita from the melancholy mood she was in. We thought it was time for Florizel to fish or cut bait on this proposal of marriage he wasn't making. So, with Thetis away, I invited him to pay us a visit. I wanted to look him in the eye and straighten things out about Perdita's lineage.

I kept looking out the front door for him. Perdita was in the kitchen. She called out, "Is there something I can get for you? Would you like a strawberry?"

I went in. I smiled. I said, "I want to explain to Florizel about you being a Sicilian royal princess and clear up his father's confusion over it."

"No, Peleus! Nothing is happening with Florizel and me. Orestes is coming back; I know it."

I didn't have the heart to break it to her. I knew every version of the Orestes story and Perdita wasn't in any of them.

"Be that as it may," I said, "I don't want it said that we are hiding anything from the King of Bohemia. Florizel is coming today, and I want everything out in the open in plain view. What you and the prince do about that is up to the two of you. So, if you need to bone up on the story of your story, now's the time to do it. He'll be here any minute."

"I know my story very well, thank you. The beginning of it, anyway; that's all we ever know. My father and Florizel's father were once best friends, until he accused him of adultery with my mother. That's how the story goes. Why open the scab of my father's jealous mistake? I don't see how anyone can straighten it out, frankly. Orestes said to let them go on thinking about me as they do. I won't go against that, and I see no reason for you to."

I said, "Perdita, if their thinking is based on a false premise, then it can only get worse, and I don't want the king misinformed. If you think there is a future for you and Orestes, you don't want that based on a false premise either. Make them equal suitors, it'll only make you stronger."

She said, "See? Even *you're* talking about a future for Orestes and me. That's a big improvement."

I sighed. "Good one; didn't see that coming. Seriously though, you should absolutely move on from Orestes because the odds are like all the stars to one strawberry."

"Peleus, that's still better than nothing. I'll take my chances."

From outside came resonant, whale-song imperatives: "Peleus, draw a bath of fresh well water! Perdita, make us hot barley tea! Throw more logs on the fire! Quick march!"

When you get marching orders from Thetis, you march.

She flung open the door, Orestes cowled over her bent shoulders like a lost lamb. Perdita rushed to him.

"Stand back Perdita, save that kiss. We need to wash off the stink first. Go soak some bandages in birchbark water for his eyes. Peleus, make a rub of sheep's oil, linden blossom, and mustard for his chest. They gave his lungs a real dose of crud. The poor boy can barely breathe, and it's been a cold ride home." She lowered Orestes to a sheepskin rug in front of the hearth. In a steady rhythm, she inhaled our mountain air and gently breathed it into his mouth.

We were all business at that point. I drew well water and warmed buckets of it on the hearth. Then, Thetis and I got him and the warm water into the wooden tub. Perdita searched the cupboards for birchbark and linden blossoms. With sea sponges that Thetis raises, I started in on a vigorous scrub like I would give a freshly shorn sheep. Pretty soon, color returned to his face. Thetis got some barley tea into him. He coughed. Oh dear Olympic gods, it was bad stuff. I needed a lot more hot water. Perdita got wet bandages around his head and eyes.

Just then there was a knock on the door. I knew who it'd be. Thetis flashed me a scowl. I unlimbered my legs and went to the door.

"Greetings, Florizel. Look, we have a situation here. I hope you don't mind waiting."

"Put him to work," Perdita shouted. "We need more water."

I looked at the crown prince of Bohemia and said, "Would you mind fetching well water, Florizel? I've got my hands full. It's an emergency."

Florizel looked at me blankly. "Really? I could ask Papa to send someone. That's a beautiful garland of heliotropes in your hair, Perdita. You look like the Queen of the May."

"Just fetch the well water, Florizel," Perdita yelled. "Give your hands blisters if you have to."

"Who's that in the tub, Perdita?"

"*Fetch!*"

I showed him how to work the well pulley. When I left him, he was struggling to bring up the first bucket. I told him I'd be right back and returned to the cottage. Perdita was distraught. Orestes had relapsed.

"He's sleeping," said Thetis. "We should put him to bed in his room. We've done all that we can for now."

I asked her, "Couldn't you get some help from your colleagues at Mount Olympus?"

"Think I haven't tried that? I'm getting chilly receptions from there. This mess involves the Furies, and no one wants to get on their bad side. This is going to take time to sort out. I think we can handle it using common sense and a lot of love."

We carried him upstairs to his room and moved the bed closer to the window. He was breathing normally. Perdita brought a chair next to the bed. She said, "You and Peleus can work on what's common sense in this situation. I'll stay here giving him lots of love."

Florizel was standing in the kitchen holding two half-full buckets of water when we returned. "Where do you want these?"

Thetis turned to me, her eyelids half up, and said, "Mmm? You brought him here?"

I said, "Just set them over by the hearth, Florizel, that's a big help. Sit down for a bit, we owe you some explaining. I'm sure you have questions."

When he had settled on the bench, he said, "Peleus, I am not a fool, and I don't like feeling like one the way I do now. I came here in good faith because you asked me to. Why are all of you so absorbed in that person?"

"He is our guest. He requires our help. We pride ourselves in hospitality to people like him."

"A stranger?"

"Not a stranger to us anymore, but, yes, even if he were a stranger."

"That is a strange custom. We are not familiar with it in our palace. I am looking forward to spending the rest of the day with Perdita. Tell her I'm expecting her."

"I'm afraid that's not going to happen, Florizel," I said.

"If I say it is then it will happen," he said. "Are you forgetting my rank?"

"I could never forget that, Florizel. But when it comes to Perdita and our guest, you do not have the full picture. That's the real reason I asked you here today, to make something clear to you and your father, the king. You see, Perdita was not born here, even though we've raised her since she was a baby. She was born in Sicily and her mother is the Queen of Sicily. Her father is—"

"Careful," Thetis whispered.

"A king," I finished. "Let's leave it at that. The point is that no matter how you look at it, Perdita is highborn and, indeed, of equal rank to you. You must inform your father of that."

Florizel slapped his palms on his knees and said, "Well done! That is splendid news. I've been having a terrible row with my dad about all this. Now this makes everything fall into place."

"Not exactly," I said. "It may change how you and the king view her rank, but it does not assure her acceptance of any marriage proposal you may have in mind but have never spoken. Perdita is very much of her own mind, and any suitor must win her by merit."

"But now she is eligible," he said.

"But that does not make her willing," I said. "She is very taken with the idea of her own free will and independence in all things."

"Where does she get that notion?"

Thetis stepped in at this point. "That brings us to the scene you witnessed here when you arrived. We have a visitor, a traveler. He was here for a month, then left, and now has returned, but in distress. He is very strong-minded about independent thinking. Perdita has grown fond of him."

Florizel reddened. "I do not recognize as a worthy rival some vagabond taken in by this farmhouse and talking nonsense to Princess Perdita! I'll challenge him to a duel and then you'll see only his backside on the run." He swept his hand in a fencer's wristy flourish.

"Watch it, Florizel," I said. "He too is a prince."

"I know all the princes. Who is he and where does he come from?"

"He is Orestes, son of Agamemnon, late of Mycenae. And he is a trained swordsman."

Florizel grew thoughtful. He fidgeted. He slapped both knees again and stood. "I have never heard of such a place. I will consult with the king and settle this once and for all when I return."

I sighed. "Very well, Florizel. I'm just glad we could have this chat. Don't be a stranger."

CHAPTER NINE

He wouldn't have made it without Perdita. He had a racking cough, and it didn't help that it rained nearly every day for a month. Thetis was attentive in a smart sort of way, but Perdita doted on him in a loving sort of way. She pulled me into his room the day after Florizel left. "Help me move his bed to the room across the hall," she said.

"Why?" he whispered.

"To get you some more sunlight!"

After that, he and Perdita shifted his bed, then his chair, from room to room to catch what little sunlight we had when the rain broke. He liked the books. He helped us understand the ones in Greek, even the ones about philosophy. He tired easily at first.

"Mother, he needs fresh fish," Perdita said to Thetis one day.

"He's too weak for fishing."

"I'm not talking about him fishing. You're not too weak for it. Couldn't you just go to an ocean and bring us back some?"

"You mean, me go to sea without a shipwreck? Just to go fishing?"

"Yes, Mother. Couldn't you just do it for me, if not for him?"

Thetis smiled and kissed Perdita's cheek. "Well, if you put it that way."

Gradually, with Thetis's fish, my shepherd's pies of mutton, and Perdita's deep-forest herbs and berries, he got his legs back. Then he could start building back muscle strength.

Last week he and Perdita returned from an afternoon walk. Thetis and I were sitting out enjoying the spring flowers and her lingonberry wine. They had gone as far as the Other Edge. They wanted to know what's on the other side of it.

"Don't go there; absolutely do not even think of going there, period," Thetis explained. "One cup of wine for you Perdita, none for you yet, Orestes. I've got lungwort tea for you. Where did you go today?"

"Not over the Other Edge," quipped Perdita. Thetis laughed.

Orestes said, "Not over it, but in sight of it. It's a nice long walk from here, and there is a grand meadow leading right up to it."

"I know that meadow very well," I said. "It's where we hold the sheep-shearing festival every year. It's too wet now but it'll be ready for the festival if the rain holds off."

"I'm ready for something like that," said Orestes, "I'm feeling stronger every day. Are there games?"

"Yes," I said, "Wrestling and stone lifting, that sort of thing."

"Archery?"

I looked at him. "Yes," I said, "If that's your sport. I don't keep bows though. I don't know how you'd practice for it."

Orestes looked away. "I've had plenty of practice recently."

Everyone fell silent.

"Will Florizel be there?" he asked.

"Very likely," I said. "But look, we use straw bales for targets, not rival princes."

He let out a healthy laugh which then became a coughing fit. He had to excuse himself. Perdita followed him with some of his syrup.

After they'd gone, I asked Thetis, "How long is that cough going to last?"

Thetis shook her head. "Just based on what I've seen with others, it could last the rest of his life. This is not a prediction, mind you. He is profoundly out of his story so I can't foresee where it's going for him specifically. I am very uncomfortable about the way he's altering his story. I worry things will go all wobbly."

"What can we do for him?"

"Well, in terms of his health, I think we've done a great deal. The problem here is the damp and the long winters. I've traveled to places that are clear and dry year-round. That would help, but I don't see how we'd organize that. He ruined all chances of returning to that kind of climate where he grew up."

I said, "Actually if they get married as they're planning, they both will be out of their stories. What do we do about that?"

Thetis shrugged, "Your guess is as good as mine. It's never happened that way before."

I leaned back. "Maybe you're being too dogmatic about the Other Edge. What if they did go over? What's the worst that can happen to them?"

"Real life."

"Hmm?"

"I mean it. It's *reality* over there. I can't tell you what that's like, Peleus. I just know that once you go you can't come back here. For me, that would mean abdicating immortality, which is fine with me, but taking on unpredictability, which is scary to me. For you, it would mean abdicating longevity and your sheep business. You'd have to find work. That means being a farmhand somewhere. But this is idle speculation. It could be entirely different. That's what scares me so."

I said, "What about just Orestes and Perdita? They're resourceful. He has his head on straight. She's well-grounded and without pretense. That should go a long way in adapting to reality, right?"

"Again, I don't know. I'm being brutally honest. The risks are unknown and could be awful. And for that very reason, I wouldn't want to let them out of my sight again. Would you?"

"What's awful?" asked Perdita.

We hadn't heard them come back downstairs. I craned my neck and looked at them. They both looked radiant. I just knew we couldn't keep them. They glowed with so much potential I knew they'd be gone somewhere soon.

"I was just telling Peleus that beyond the Other Edge would be awful," Thetis muttered.

"How do you know, Thetis? I thought you'd never been there," said Orestes.

"Orestes, your raw rationality is going to land you in trouble. Just accept the wisdom of your elders," said Thetis.

Orestes said, "No, I never intend to contradict you, Thetis. I admire you a great deal and owe you much more. Your wisdom, and the wisdom of other elders, I will always welcome. That's as it should be. My concern—my objection—is living a storyline written by others, who might be less wise than I am."

I spoke up, "Orestes, there are gods, kings, masters, and proprietors. You cannot change the order of things. Are you suggesting equal autonomy for all? All foot soldiers and no generals?"

He said, "No, not that. I'm talking about forced ranking for a lifetime; unearned and unconsented to autonomy of others, even a storyteller. That is more than autonomy, it is ownership, and the owned are always treated as less than human."

I said, "But Orestes, the fact of the matter is that you are a creature of your storyteller. That's who has your future all mapped out. You cannot go around changing your story."

Perdita looked at me. "I'm not so sure about that, Peleus. If that were the case, the Fold would have just one Edge. But it is double-edged. Just because you and Mother haven't gone beyond the Other Edge doesn't mean the other side is without purpose. And it must be accessible to us because it's there, in plain sight."

Alarmed, I said, "Thetis has always said 'don't go there.'"

"It is mysterious and unknown," Perdita said. "For an immortal goddess and a king with guaranteed longevity, it can only go downhill in another world. But you can't discount the possibility that Orestes and I might be better off to flee the jurisdiction."

Thetis sighed. "She does have a point."

No one spoke as we thought about it. From the trees behind the cottage came the songs of birds on their evening foraging. The shadows deepened gradually. Bells on the sheep grew quiet as they sank to the grass for the night. From the hillside, a flute imitated a cuckoo, descended in thirds and sevenths, then eased into a waltz. I shook my head slowly and wondered, *Why would anyone trade here for anywhere else?*

Orestes stood up and gathered empty cups. "When is this sheep-shearing festival, Peleus? I need to step up my fitness routine."

"Six weeks, Orestes. It's always fun. Everyone involved in sheep ranching and the wool trade will be there. You need to bring an appetite and a thick skin—there's a lot of rude teasing going on."

"Six weeks. Great. I can take and give tease."

CHAPTER TEN

The day of the festival came. Perdita and I were in the kitchen early. She was in a lavender blouse, a leaf-green dirndl, and wore mayflowers woven in the braids encircling her head.

Orestes skipped down the stairs and into the kitchen. Perdita yelped.

"Orestes, put some clothes on," I said.

"This is how Achaean men go to the games," he said with a shrug.

"That'll just get you thirty days in an uncomfortable jail here. Get dressed. Your work clothes will be fine," I said.

"Too confining. How about the tunic?"

Perdita stifled a laugh. "You'd look like a girl."

"And 'Florizel' sounds like a girl," he said.

A trumpet sounded. Then came a knock on the door. "Oyez, the cottage, attend! Prince Florizel shall be pleased to put a question to Maid Perdita!"

I looked out the window. *Oh my.* Florizel looked diminutive astride a black warhorse. The mount's reins were held by the herald with the trumpet and loud voice. Standing a few yards away, a white stallion pawed the ground, ridden by a tall, white-haired man, dressed as a clown.

I turned back and shouted, "The tunic, then, but hurry. Perdita, go to the door."

Perdita stood in the doorway, trying to think of an appropriate greeting. "Question?"

"May I please use the…? It's urgent."

Perdita pointed to the privy, downwind from the henhouse, and looked away modestly as Florizel dismounted and hastened there.

She walked to the man on the white horse. "Sir Clown, would you care to come in for something to drink?"

The lanky man in his sixties, dressed in multicolored harlequin tights and a scarlet mask, answered, "That is kind. However, since I rarely ride these days, I'd rather not have to dismount."

"I'll bring it to you."

"No need, Maid Perdita, but stay and tell me of you. What most pleases you?"

"The sky, starry nights, the sounds of the forest, and flowers, Sir Clown."

"Two are permanent, two are not; two are simple, two are not," he replied.

"All are simple at first, then change, Sir Clown. Flower blossoms and night sounds do so more quickly."

"Which flowers?"

Perdita touched thumb to fingers as she said, "Lamb's ears, bluebells, sweet woodruff—"

"Red poppies?" suggested the clown.

She added, "Yes, and disheveled iris heads, bleeding hearts, and white foxglove."

She paused with her head downward and away. The clown said, "Is that all you remember?"

She turned and exclaimed, "Rosemary for remembrance!"

The clown nodded gravely. "Well read and well-remembered; the aftertaste of grief."

"Thank you. And you? What do you fancy?"

"Everything that is fancy, girl. An ornate portrait in a carved frame, complex cuisine, an agile dance, a well-seated castle, a tapestry of history."

Perdita said, "Those are high art and complicated artifacts. I live a simpler life. But is a clown's life complicated? I would not have thought so."

"Think again. Looks deceive. 'Simple at first,' as you say, 'then, change.' You have said it correctly; will you live it so? Ah, here comes the prince, looking much relieved."

"Will you go now, Sir Clown?"

"We go to the festival. Is it far?"

"I have walked to its meadow. Yours will be a short ride from here."

"Will you walk there today, Maid Perdita?"

"I shall, with my family."

"Your cottage, your family, all may appear pastoral and common. But you, Maid Perdita, are no commoner, are you? How ever came your birth, today your thoughts are high and complicated, Maid Perdita: nature, art, and life. I expect we shall speak of them again and often as things change for you from low to high."

Perdita again looked down and away, blushing. "Your praises are too large, Sir Clown."

The clown bent to reach into a leather pouch. He pulled a long rosemary sprig from the pouch, sniffed it, and tossed it to her. "There will come a time I'd hope you remember me on this day."

He nudged the white horse ahead.

Florizel came to Perdita's side. He said, "You will see more of him today and for many days. I know of your rank, Princess. Today, in front of all your rude countrymen, he shall proclaim our union. Once that is done, it cannot be undone and cannot be denied. Please wear a cheerful smile then, though I do not see it now."

With the herald's help, Florizel remounted and followed the clown. The herald walked behind. Perdita returned to us in the cottage.

"Who's your new friend?" Orestes asked, now in his white tunic with purple trim.

"A clown. He did not say his name."

Thetis sighed, "He didn't need to, Perdita. Do you not know who he is?"

"I know he is gentle."

"He is Polixenes, King of Bohemia." Thetis blinked; a salty tear filled her eye.

At that, Perdita collapsed to the rough wooden floor, her hands over her face, realizing the meaning of his words. She trembled and her shoulders shook. She lifted her head, her cheeks flushed and tear-streaked, "Now I am truly lost. Orestes, take me to Mycenae. Why did I hesitate before? Take me there. I shall go where you go. Your people shall be my people."

Orestes sank to his knees beside her. "We will go, but not to the House of Atreus. That is crumbling beyond repair. I am unwilling to wage the necessary wars to replace it. Our fate is certain and dire if we return. Thetis says my story in Mycenae is over. I was there and saw that more than just a story had ended.

I sense a dark history approaching my homeland. There must be a better way."

"What way?" she moaned.

Orestes shrugged. "It is simple, as you like to say. If not here and if not over the Edge, then we will simply choose to go over the Other Edge."

Thetis started, "I don't know…"

Orestes turned to her, "I know you don't. That won't stop us. No one knows what's even around the corner. We will find out today. Are you two ready to come with us? To the festival, I mean."

"Give us a moment, please," I said. I took Thetis aside. She was subdued. We looked around the room at the familiar iron-ware, crocks, pewter pitchers, and dishware. We were thinking the same thing.

I said to Thetis, "I never thought I'd ever say this to you, but we should go too. They are not equipped for this alone. We have a lovely life here, but I feel we are just treading water."

She smiled. "I'm an expert at that."

"If we go with them, we would have a purpose. If we stayed, we'd never stop worrying about them. Whatever we did here would seem unfulfilling. She is our baby."

"We can't live their lives for them," she said.

"Of course. But we can be near them, at least I hope so."

"Hope is about all you have to go on, Peleus. I am in the dark completely. We might arrive somewhere near, or we might turn up far away from them and each other, even in different epochs. But I agree with your feelings completely. I hate to think about adding eternal concern over them on top of the eternal grief I already suffer for Achilles."

"So, it's settled?" I asked.

"It is settled that I cannot bear parting from them. I cannot disown my love for them."

"Can you bear parting with the Fold?" I asked.

"The Fold will go on unchanged. Zeus will simply find another couple to run it."

"You're sure?"

"I checked it with him," she said. "I saw this coming, Peleus. I say we go where they go."

"Should we pack?"

Thetis shrugged, "For what? I have no idea where we'll land. And I don't want to drag our bags all the way to the meadow."

CHAPTER ELEVEN

The meadow is an open space covered in wildflowers, through which a broad stream meanders in a great horseshoe bend, shouldered with willows and oleanders. Beyond the outer bank of the bend, the ground rises to meet ancient trees and ferns, except for one wide spot where the clearing just terminates. Behind the terminus is a strange structure—strange even when compared to the strangeness of the black-edged, rainbow-colored Fold itself. It reaches from the ground into the sky, higher than the clouds. It is a matte-finished, metallic barrier with two vertical slits, spaced fairly closely together. Each of the slits, while appearing narrow in relation to the rest of the strange structure, would easily admit a full-sized adult man or woman. There is a gap of nothingness on the far side of the slitted plate, and beyond that is a back screen—non-metallic, of indeterminate composition. When light from the Fold passes through the slits and hits the back screen, profoundly unpredictable chiaroscuro scatter patterns appear there that defy logic. The gap between the double-slitted plate and the back screen is vast, its fearsome drop seemingly bottomless. Half a dozen sheep dogs sit in a line at the brink of the clearing to turn stray sheep from wandering over what everyone calls the Other Edge.

Shepherds drive their families' flocks of sheep along the dusty road to where it widens and ends near the bend in the stream. Its horseshoe encloses a flat grassy area large enough to hold an arbored pavilion, nearly two hundred sheep, and racks to hold their shorn wool. Boys and dogs herd the sheep through the wide, shallow stream for a wash before the shearing by older boys and adults. Near the pavilion, on ground littered with cast-off red and green cabbage leaves, women at makeshift wooden stalls serve water gathered in large vats the day before, when the stream was clear. Others serve thick beer or fruity wine from skins, clay jugs, and barrels. The pavilion holds a pick-up band with players of uneven talents on lutes, recorders, and various handheld hoops of tightly drawn skin—tambor drums. Some drummers tap rhythms with sticks, others just make beats with fingers and palms. In front of the pavilion stands a ten-foot may-pole adorned with wide streamers.

For us, the trick had always been to get on the road as early as possible to avoid the inevitable delays from ambling sheep and heavy pushcarts. Today's impromptu royal visit and its aftermath put us at the peak of foot traffic on the road to the meadow, lined with the white and purple lilacs of May. We made our plans as we made our way through dust clouds, bell clanks, whistles, and barks. When we arrived at the meadow, we had fashioned a plan.

Before you see the meadow, you smell the roasting pits. The first things you hear are the dogs, then the blended sounds of the stream and peals of laughter. When we arrived, Perdita tried to fluff away the accumulated dust from her dirndl. Thetis tried to put away her apprehensions. Perdita joined other girls gathering on the grass near the maypole in gaudy dresses and performing circle dances. Their laughter joined with a hurdy-gurdy's droning melodies. It reminded me and other elders of storied dances of Druids in fables. I thought, *Music of paradise! Will I ever hear it again?*

Orestes jogged straight to the part of the field where the games were going on. I watched him pick up various sized stones to try them out. Apart from the rowdy crowd stood a slender, multi-colored tent and a skinny pennant on a bent pole. One black and one white horse grazed on clover and columbine, flanks twitching away noisy flies. Florizel and the clown sat silently watching everyone else's fun.

Orestes picked up two stones and walked to the royal tent.

"Florizel, care to join me? The distance stone putting is for teams of two. I have no partner. Might you make a team of it with me?"

The clown smiled and looked away, waiting for his son's response. Florizel's tardy assent came in a voice that revealed insecurity, and his face revealed discomfort. As they proceeded to the games field, I smiled and saluted Polixenes with two fingers at my brow. He nodded and removed the red mask to show his smile in return. I put down my shears and followed the boys.

Orestes showed Florizel the basic mechanics of the stone toss. Scoring was simple: the combined distances of teams of two. Orestes' impressive throws kept them in the lead despite the weaker ones by Florizel. But competing as a team made for a conspicuous display of their differences, and such was not to Florizel's advantage. He began to fume in frustration with every cheer for their team.

He snarled when they had won, "Orestes, will you compete against me with something sharper than stones?"

"Gladly. May I pick the game?"

"That is the custom of this challenge."

Orestes said, "I choose bow and arrow, targets at increasing distances. Did you bring such weapons?"

"Of course, what prince wouldn't?"

"We shall both use the same—yours—for the sake of fairness," said Orestes with a smile.

Florizel sent the herald scampering back to the lonely tent for the bow and arrows. There, the clown whispered to the herald and pointed to the maypole. The herald nodded. He returned to Florizel with a bow and two quivers of ten arrows each. Then he set off to find Perdita.

She and three other girls were in a line in front of the pavilion, backs straight, heads high, elbows bent to make circles, and rising tip-toe to the rhythm of a lute. The herald stood waiting until the music stopped and Perdita relaxed back on her heels. The herald pointed to her. She turned to face him. He bowed and beckoned her to follow. She looked at the solitary royal tent and saw the clown standing alone next to the crooked pennant pole. She stepped to a wooden counter, collected two mugs of water, and followed the herald.

"You must have some water, your... um... Your Honor, Noble Majesty, Sire..."

"'Sir Clown' suits me and was comfortable for you before. Stick with that."

"Thank you, Sir Clown. You wanted to see me?"

"*Again*. I wanted to see you again."

"Have you thought of another flower for our list?"

"My son is a nice boy, well brought up. He's fond of you."

"And you, Sir Clown?"

"Growingly so, but Sicilia is more our focus. I will announce his betrothal to you today."

"Yet, he has not asked me for it, nor have you. You both have simply declared it."

"Florizel should have, I acknowledge that. Were he to do so, what would be your reply?"

"You do not want to hear my reply, if he had chosen to ask."

The clown smiled broadly and stretched his long arms out to the side, "There! You see? That is why neither of us has asked. You favor simple things; nothing is simpler for royalty than to declare, rather than request."

Perdita curtseyed. "I am learning that, Sir Clown. It leaves simple folk with uncomfortable choices."

King Polixenes frowned but said nothing. Then, "Thank you for the water. The fact is, your thoughtful generosity, served with candor and directness, makes my next choice very uncomfortable."

Perdita bowed low. "Then you should rest, Sir Clown, in your shaded tent. Good day to you." She turned to go.

"Wait. I could call off the announcement. I could speak to Florizel."

Perdita turned back. "In that case would you announce my betrothal to Orestes?"

"That would be uncomfortable for me, Maid Perdita."

"Is that because I am Princess Perdita?"

"Yes, exactly. It would be a public afront to my son."

"Rest well, King Polixenes, I believe we understand each other completely."

At the archery range, things were going badly for Florizel. As his arrows missed their marks, even at close range, Florizel grew tight in the shoulders and red in the face. Orestes, on the other hand, was in good spirits from his successes and the appreciative applause he was winning from the bystanders.

When Perdita arrived, she threw kisses to Orestes as she clapped for him. Thetis joined her, holding a pouch filled with mutton from the roasting pits, a big part of her plan, although she never eats meat.

Florizel finally roared in outrage. He hurled the bow, not to the ground, but straight at Orestes. The point of one tip of the bow struck Orestes' right shoulder, drawing blood. Orestes whirled to face the Prince of Bohemia, scowling and surprised. Florizel unsheathed his hand-and-a-half sword, gripped its cruciform hilt, and touched Orestes' damp shoulder with the tip of its straight, double-edged, thirty-five–inch blade.

"You? A prince? Then, doubtful prince, we shall skip the frolic and games, and you shall meet the soothing edges of this blade in a combat worthy of men, not boys," Florizel snarled.

Perdita gasped and shouted, "Florizel, he cannot fight! He has been sick for weeks with a strange contagion!"

Florizel laughed, "'Strange,' she calls it? Strange, indeed, that the meek lamb needs three people to bathe it. Strange? No, exceedingly convenient is what I call it, if you now declare him incapable of manly challenge."

Orestes shrugged, smiled, and said, "I have no sword, Florizel."

"Then you are no prince!" the challenger roared. Again, he jabbed Orestes, this time in the center of his chest. Orestes winced but stood firm.

Florizel taunted him, "Well, well, a swordless royal. Perhaps there is nothing hard and pointed in his physique as well." This time Florizel jabbed Orestes below the belt. The bystanders groaned in disapproval.

"See if you can borrow a blade of some sort from all these friends of yours," sneered Florizel. "But, if swordless, then you are pointless, Orestes. And if you are pointless, you are worthless to a princess. You should run, or hop, or limp, as your malady allows, back to your sheep."

Orestes said, "I am content to stand. I shall leave this field when Perdita and I are good and ready. Your sword is your crutch, Florizel. Put it away, you won't want to stain it. So, too, are your words. You take satisfaction from hearing the taunts of your own tongue and from watching meagre drippings of my blood. I'll gladly fight you swordless."

Florizel fumed. "Meagre? Then, I must make you more generous in your drippings, false prince."

This time Florizel's sword tip sliced Orestes from hand and wrist to his elbow, again drawing blood and gasps from the onlookers. Orestes clamped his other hand to the wound to stanch the bleeding and twisted to one side. Florizel then jabbed his sword point at the calf of Orestes' leg, just above his heel. Orestes took one hop on his other foot, turned back, and stood firm. I was proud to see his self-control.

But, I became alarmed when Florizel raised the point of his sword to Orestes' throat. Orestes remained still. Florizel's eyes narrowed. He gritted his teeth and made to lunge!

Florizel held his sword with the sharp edges at the vertical; better practice would be to hold its blade flat, sharp edges on the horizontal. Orestes windmilled his injured arm against the flat of the blade. He surged forward on his uninjured leg to deliver a left jab to the bridge of Florizel's nose. Florizel's weapon spun harmlessly to the side and his nose dripped generously of the royal blood. Orestes crouched, prepared for hand-to-hand combat. Stunned, Florizel fell to the ground and groped blindly for his sword.

But it was no longer on the ground. When his eyes cleared, he saw that it now rested on an arm covered in harlequin checks. King Polixenes, face unmasked and stern, stood in the stirrups of his high, white horse. His herald stood next to him holding the reins of the black warhorse.

"Enough!" the king barked.

"I need my sword!" Florizel screamed.

"Not to get what we need," declared the king for all to hear. "We'd get nowhere with your swordsmanship. All you need to acquire the princess and her island is my decree!"

"*Now!*" shouted Thetis, in her deepest voice that wakens distant whales. "Enough is indeed *enough!*"

Surprise had been the plan, and her timing surprised even Orestes, Perdita, and me.

We turned and made for the hill. At this point, Orestes was limping badly. Perdita slid under one of his arms and helped him up the hill.

A cry went up from below. After we reached the crest of the hill, I turned to assess reactions. My eyes were fixed on the royals. The herald helped Florizel mount the black warhorse. With Florizel's whoop and whipping reins, the horse set off across the stream in an eruption of spray. The horse lunged closer.

As we approached the crest of the clearing, the sheep dogs gathered, barking. Thetis handed Orestes her pouch of cooked meat, which had also been a part of the plan. Orestes calmed the dogs a bit with quiet words as he flung chunks of mutton to distract them further. We struggled to the Other Edge. The four of us stood together, out of breath, staring at the inexplicable double-slitted structure.

The warhorse labored up the slope. Florizel, having lost his challenge, then his face, and now his prospects for both a bride and the kingdom of Sicily, croaked profanities in hateful, jealous fury, his eyes ablaze.

Orestes threw back his head and roared out a Mycenean battle cry. Then, in single file, he, Perdita, and Thetis leapt through one of the slits. The dogs turned their attention to the horse, now at full gallop. They crouched together, snarling and barking, teeth bared, causing the charging horse to balk and throw its rider. Florizel went tumbling over headfirst, vainly trying to stop himself before he somersaulted into the other slit.

I took one last look at the Fold, turned, and hurled myself after my family over the Other Edge.

THE OTHER EDGE

"The king shall live without an heir, if
that which is lost be not found."

—WILLIAM SHAKESPEARE,
The Winter's Tale (Act III, Scene II)

"Art must take reality by surprise…not
pose the 'real' as a preoccupation."

—FRANCOISE SAGAN, "The Art of Fiction No. 15"

CHAPTER TWELVE

No longer was I lost, nor was I named Perdita. I was Sophie, a gloriously common name. No longer did I have unseen parentage. I was of solid Bohemian stock, the proud Chotek family. I found myself on a train, in new skin, twenty-four years old, three centuries later, in July 1892. I had dozed off. The carriage was hot, as was my dress.

My head began to clear. The noisy clamor of barking dogs and hoofbeats in my dream gave way to the clacking of the rails. I felt reasonably happy except that I longed for a certain man from my past, or from my dreams. I just knew that he was someone I had once been with but now I had lost. I must have known him on a rural property before I moved to Vienna for a job. I had not given up hope of reuniting with him. Other memories would come and go in my mind, especially the short woman with roseate eyes and gifted with foresight whom I sometimes called "Mother" in my dreams.

Across the carriage from me slumped an ample woman, perspiring, asleep and heavily mouth-breathing over an open picnic basket. I thought, *she is…um…yes, of course, my very own employer, Princess Isabella of Croy.* Next to her sat her pretty daughter,

Archduchess Maria Christina, holding a crumpled telegram in one hand and a busy fan in the other.

The telegram invited Isabella and Maria Christina to a shooting party at Pressburg, Hungary. We were on our way there from Isabella's country residence, Halbturn Castle, southeast of Vienna. I thought, *Isabella will be hunting for some promising aristocrat for her daughter to marry, while he, whoever he may be, and his comrades will be hunting for some timid, frightened forest animals to kill.* I was on my way there to wait. It's what ladies-in-waiting do, and what Isabella employed me to do between instructions.

Ah well. It was certainly a beautiful day to visit my sister, Maria Pia, and her husband, Jaroslav. It was at their lodge where all the game slaughter would take place. You'd think that my family's invitation to her might have caused Isabella to treat me more as a friend than a fetch-maid, but you'd be mistaken to do so.

Isabella bounced awake when the train rumbled over a timber trestle. She looked around and saw that I was resting, thus requiring instructions.

"Did you remember to bring a newspaper, Sophie?"

I nodded and reached into the picnic basket I had packed for her travel elevenses. I dusted away breadcrumbs from the folded newspaper and opened it. On the front page was the etching of an exotic Asian woman in silk robes near a mountain stream. The etching's caption said: "...the signing in June of a treaty of friendship, trade and navigation, and diplomatic relations between the Empire and the Kingdom of Corea." I handed the newspaper to Isabella who studied the etching. She frowned silently. I could imagine her thoughts: *pretty, but it wouldn't fit me.* She passed the paper to her daughter. I felt sure that she was thinking the same thing.

Maria Christina said, "That was weeks ago. Why are they printing that now?"

Isabella whispered importantly, "Probably as a distraction from the real news, which is a secret treaty with Russia and Germany."

Maria shrugged, "If it's a secret, how do you know it?"

"Well, dear, you know it now. Feel free to use it to impress Archduke Franz Ferdinand at dinner tonight."

The train's whistle pierced my ears, and we entered a tunnel. It was after dark by the time we arrived at the hunting lodge. Isabella went straight to bed upon our arrival.

EARLY THE NEXT MORNING, my sister watched me unpack, straighten, and hang the wardrobes of Isabella and Maria Christina. I knew it pained her to watch me carrying out the chores of a maid. It pained us both to reminisce about mother and father. Wilhelmine had died four years earlier. Our father, Count Bohuslav Chotek, was unwell.

My memory-mother, Thetis, had forty-nine sisters to my none. I always envied her for at least one but kept it to myself for fear of seeming small-minded. In my Chotek family, I finally got an abundance of sisters. Too many as it turned out. Because of our noble Bohemian house, the girls all got the title "Countess." But, after Father provided dowries for Anna, Maria Pia, Karolina, and Henriette, there was nothing left for Zdenka and me. Although he had tried to entice men for us, he could offer them nothing.

Anyway, none of them interested me. I knew what I wanted but had yet to find the man of my dreams. So, at twenty, it was a simple choice for me when Mama Wilhelmine died: I looked for employment. Father was saddened and embarrassed. I was not—I had to be practical. I still kept and revered the now-dry sprigs of rosemary he gave me when I left home for service in Vienna as lady-in-waiting to Isabella.

A shotgun blasted close to the house. I jumped.

Maria Pia said, "Don't be alarmed, it's a practice shot. They can't seem to wait until the hunt begins."

I said to her, "Maria Pia, tonight, at table, I'm to sit with you, if that's all right."

"Yes, of course, that's perfect."

"I agree. Normally I would be with Isabella and Maria Christina, but Isabella has her eye on the prize: to entangle her daughter with the heir presumptive. For that, she'll entrap Archduke Franz Ferdinand to sit between them."

Maria Pia smiled, "Oh, I do know. She made that very plain to me when she asked to be invited. Do you know the Archduke now that you are in Vienna society?"

"I'm hardly that, as you can plainly see. I wouldn't know him if I saw him. How about you?"

Maria Pia shrugged. "He's hunted here before. He hunts incessantly. He keeps to himself. Your Isabella is not the first to dangle a daughter in front of him. He never takes the bait."

"Oh, no!" I laughed.

Maria Pia leaned closer. "He arrived just before you did. He rises early and raids the pantry. He may very well be snacking downstairs already. Why don't you go down there and…?"

"Don't be ridiculous," I said.

"I'm not being ridiculous, Sophie Chotek! I know you. Why do you think I was so easy for Isabella to persuade? I can play that game as well as she. He can sometimes appear abrupt, but don't let his chilly exterior put you off."

I had unfolded enough of others' garments for the day. "Hmm. You are a wicked conspirator."

"Go."

CHAPTER THIRTEEN

I felt his eyes explore me. When he saw me glance at him, he turned away and studied one of the draperies. He coughed lightly. His face was flushed. His hair didn't seem right. It was straight for one thing, thick and black. The gentle moss of a mustache now was part of foliage above and below the mouth and right up the sides of his face. I was almost sure, but not quite.

I went to the hunt board and searched for...*ah, there they are!* With a silver slotted spoon, I placed them on a white porcelain dish edged in purple and said, "Care for a fig?"

His fingers touched mine as he took one. I picked another from the plate and held it to his lips. He trembled. Softly he said, "No."

"No?" I was stunned.

He said, "It can't be. You can't be. You aren't, are you?" He turned his head, covered his face, and coughed again, this time in labored, deep, turbulence.

The cough ignited strong, vibrant, long-ago memories. Suddenly the memories soared in my mind like a hot-air balloon inflating throughout my head. These memories blurred in and out at the edges of other memories of my life, as if I could remember two lives at once.

I placed my hand against his cheek. *My dream, now in trousers not meant for farm work.* His eyes were watery. His chest heaved. I knew every nuance of his breathing. There could be no doubt: it was he. My heart was on fire. Now, my search was over. But could I keep him? I said,

"Whom do you see?"

"I see a dream," he said. "I thought I'd lost you.'"

"I'm Sophie," I said.

"You always wanted—"

"Yes, I know, and Sophie is an incredibly common name. Have you seen Thetis?" I asked.

"She arrived here over thirty years ago, much younger, a teen-ager, about the age you and I were when—"

"I would like to see her!" I exclaimed. "What does she do?"

"Anything she wants to, Sophie. She became Elisabeth, Empress of Austria and Queen of Hungary, wife of Emperor Franz Josef. You wouldn't recognize her. When you do see her, call her Sissi; we all do. I think it's because she's the younger sister of the girl the emperor was supposed to marry but instead fell instantly in love with Sissi. They were married four days later."

My head was spinning with confusing memory swirls. I knew the name of the empress, of course, every schoolgirl does, but I never made the connection. "Then, is she your mother? You are the emperor's son?"

"No, they are uncle and aunt. Here, let me explain." He picked up a bowl of yellow apples from the hunt board and placed on the table one for each name in a chart as he recited:

"Then thus:

The Holy Roman Emperor,
Francis the Second, and Napoleon
Battled back and forth till one held France,
The other barely clung to Austria.
Kaiser Francis Second's third-born son,
Archduke Franz Karl, had four sons,
The first, Franz Josef, and Sissi, had but one,
Rudolph, but he and Stephanie had none.
The second, Max, the King of Mexico,
Was shot by Juarez rifle squad one dawn.
The third, Karl Ludwig and Wife Two had me,
The fourth one never wanted any wife.
Rudolph shot his mistress and himself
In their heads, in his bed, 'midst scarlet flowers.
The crown next would go to Dad, but he's
Sixty, typhoid sickly, and professes
Not to want the job of emperor,
So, in time it goes…"

He laid two apples last in line, side by side, and kissed me.

"…To us and ours."

I said, "I am one of eight children of Count Bohuslav Chotek of Bohemia and Wilhelmine Kinsky of Germany. My line, if I were to draw it with apples, would reach through three and a half centuries of strong Bohemian aristocrats faithful to the Habsburg dynasty. They served, not sought, the crown. I serve now as lady-in-waiting to Princess Isabella of Croy."

A searing question burst to the front of my brain, deep from my memory.

"Sir, I well know you are keen to rule a domain. Must I again become one of two difficult choices: kingdom or love? You and I have had an impossible transformation and still we meet again. If your love for me is true, take me away now. Let's not go through another revolving door between crown and love."

He stiffened and shook his head. "I am no different today from when you last knew me. My most important thing in life is reuniting with you and living what remains of my life with your love. Do not treat rule and love as irreconcilable."

"Did you get a better mother?"

"Maria Annunziata of Bourbon-Two Sicilies."

"Two of them? You don't mean my mother—again!"

"One Sicily, but there was a mainland merger of sorts. And, again, your mother is not in the picture. But for me, two mothers. My mother married my father by proxy, then died when I was eight. His third wife raised me: Maria Theresa is Mama to me. Yes, this time I got a better mother. Do you play tennis well?"

"I do not," I replied with smile. In fact, I did, but I did not want to boast. "You have changed the subject. I have watched at the tennis court of Halbturn Castle. I have thwacked tennis balls aimlessly against a wall there but have not attempted actual games. Should I?"

"Yes. That way opens more possibilities."

"Why tennis? Are there no haylofts in your realm? Bedrooms in your castles?"

He cleared his throat. "I need to look into some process issues, imperial court administrivia."

I picked up three of the smallest apples from the bowl and spaced them in a line below the last two he had set. I said, "I must ask again: is wearing the crown the most important thing in your life? You speak of heirs like they are apple tree scions, heirs in endless succession. Look at the apple chart now. Tell me, what do you see?"

"I see a second chance for the second time. I see a dream fulfilled."

"Babies! Tell me you see uncrowned babies, Archduke! Babies dependent upon our love and care and who never desire for more than that from you and me."

Just then Isabella and Maria Christina stepped into the entry-way at the same time. Isabella exclaimed. I looked away from the Archduke to watch mother and daughter surge, stop, and start again, this time with Isabella in the lead. Her haste caused her to wobble.

As he stepped to help steady her, he whispered to me, "One step at a time. Tennis first."

Isabella took the Archduke's hand and shook it vigorously. He reached for me, but I had stepped closer to the tall windows, trying to catch my breath. I was shaking. It began to rain.

THE DINNER, UNSURPRISINGLY, FEATURED upland game bird seasoned with buckshot. With it, Maria Pia's kitchen served creamed onions, winter squash, potatoes with sausage, and beets. The Archduke gamely engaged in Vienna gossip with Isabella and Maria Christina. But he went dark and gruff when Maria

Christina mentioned talks among the empire, Russia, and Germany. He stiffened, threw his napkin on his plate, and quickly left the table. Maria blushed heavily and scowled at her mother. Isabella became flustered. She rose and beckoned to me. I followed Princess Isabella upstairs and tended to her preparations for bed.

I was crushed. I might never have a chance like this again. If so, it must be because he makes it so.

CHAPTER FOURTEEN

The first letter to arrive had two envelopes, one fitted into the other, both with addresses, and delivered by footman. Mine read,

> *Dear Lost and Found,*
> *Until there is a better way, the written word shall be our way.*
> *Deliver the enclosed to your mistress. Expect more to you from,*
> *I don't know, new names, imaginary names; just know the*
> *spirit behind the names. Be my…tennis partner.*
>
> *Always,*
> *Baron von Barnyard*

I took the other envelope to Isabella with her morning white, sugared tea on a silver charger and an ivory letter opener. She studied it and her eyes widened. Her lip trembled. She ignored the letter opener and tore away the flap which fell to the floor.

> *My compliments to the Exquisite Princess Isabella,*
> *It is with deep regret and trembling hand that I write to*
> *express apologies for my mysterious exit during our sparkling*

*conversation at dinner at the lodge. I had a sudden spasm. I
often suffer a clutching at the chest. It is a chronic and annoy-
ing friend—I should say an enemy—who resides in my lungs.
Much as I wanted to reply to the astute insights offered by your
well-informed daughter on matters of State, I simply could not
express myself. When such spells occur my best remedy is to find
solitude in which to allow my old enemy to exhaust himself
through coughing. I can only aspire to a second opportunity (do
I dare say many more?) to revive our conversation, although
Maria Christina's political insights may simply overshadow
anything I may say. Please, do consider favorably my plea
for another chance. Let it be soon since in a few weeks I will
depart for a lengthy voyage to tropical ports of call where the
climate may be inhospitable to the enemy of my lungs.*

Your servant,
Franz Ferdinand

She let the letter slip from her hand to the floor. She turned
to me. "Sophie, bring me my diary. We need to schedule an inti-
mate dinner with an important personage, and to organize it
with great urgency."

I was thrilled. We looked through her Christmas calendar.
There were a great many open dates. She agonized over each possibility. We settled on the first Saturday of December. Isabella went
to work making drafts of a handwritten invitation. I picked up the
letter and stifled a laugh as I read it.

*But, to which barn would I address my own reply? There are so
many stables of the royal household. I need a new dress.*

FOUR BLACK HORSES DREW an ornate, low-slung, gold gilt carriage to the Palais Erzherzog Albrecht, home of Archduke Friedrich, Duke of Teschen, and his wife, my employer, Isabella. Archduke Franz Ferdinand stepped from the carriage and into the wide entryway of the austere, white, three-storied building. A footman took the Archduke's steel-blue cloak and stiff, billed hat.

I stood nearby holding a porcelain plate edged in pale yellow and decorated with three breaching gray dolphins. The plate held a compote of quinces, plums, and figs. He took the plate with a smile. He studied its decoration, then looked at me.

"Dolphins? In Vienna?"

I curtseyed.

He said with a twinkle, "This service belongs to Empress Elisabeth. Did your mistress abscond with it?"

"One with a perverted and suspicious mind might think so, sir," I said. "I suggested that she borrow the plates for tonight's occasion. Sissi is a legend among women."

He leaned closer, "And, you know the significance of the dolphin emblems."

I looked downward and away. "How could I not? Her sea escapades and uncommon affection for dolphins are also legends."

"She now is tall and slender. Her eyes are like yours and mine, only a deep, sea blue. She now rides horses, not dolphins—a champion equestrienne. You will know her independent spirit, of course. I must take you to her one day so that you may hear her tell her own legends."

"I would be so very grateful for the chance to see her—"

"Again," he finished.

I curtseyed again.

"Capital idea! I'll take you to her just as soon as I return from this voyage she talked me into taking."

"How long will you be away?" My voice quavered.

"I leave in two weeks. I'm to be away very nearly a year, I'm afraid. I'm off to hot and dry climates for my health, and to Asia, Canada, and America for the empire's diplomatic health. By the time I return I expect you to be proficient at tennis."

"And I shall make your syrup of my native land, from a recipe from before time. You shall need it every day. I shall be busy, but you shall have enough."

"You mustn't burden—"

"Of course, I must. Again."

Isabella approached with Maria Christina. The moment was over. The Archduke extended his arm to Maria Christina. Isabella led them to the dining room. I stepped away and tried to fade into the gold-trimmed French blue paneling.

OVER THE MONTHS THAT followed I came to know the footman who now stood at the tradesman's entrance of the Palais Albrecht. In silence he handed me a letter. In silence I handed him more vials to forward to India, and coins and strudel for him to keep. In the solitude of my chambers, I read:

SMS Kaiserin Elisabeth at Port Said

Dear Lost Lamb,
Since my family saw me off in Trieste, I have felt a crushing homesickness. Oh, Lamb, not nostalgia for Vienna but the

painful homesickness of separation from you and the nearest hayloft. I faithfully swallow exact measurements of your syrup daily. I treasure its vials more than the captain of this vessel does his seaborne cache of vintage wines.

Our vessel is two years old, the newest of the fleet's warships, and named for Sissi! Isn't that so appropriate for my passage through the waters of Greece? I persuaded the captain to steer as close as our draft would allow in the wine-dark bay of Argive's southeast coast. I recognized a certain estuary and rocky promontory. The sudden rush of memories crashed upon me afresh. The sensations confined me to my stateroom that night and next day. Which is the more incredible: that I was rescued from death there or that I passed by it again, hale and hearty, on a steel-hulled cruiser named for my rescuer?

I send this from Egypt. Your packet of syrup was delivered in good order and much appreciated. Ahead lies India and my nemesis: the English language. I shall have to be on my best behavior to make up for inevitable gaffes in speaking with my British hosts.

My companion, Franz Janaczek, sends warm regards. Ah, you think you do not know him. But, Lamb, you are so very wrong about that. You are to be forgiven to not recognize the name. But you know very well the spirit of the man, as gentle as a shepherd and as wise as any king who ever ruled. He showed up as the gamekeeper at my Konopischt castle. I seldom get out there, but I hope to change that in future. He presented himself to me in its rose garden some time ago. He is now about our age! He and I are companions. He is both friend and mentor. I always turn to him when I need advice. This voyage would be a dreary one were he not here for companionship and conversation. I look forward to bringing us all together soon.

I must board. I end this letter in haste in the harbor master's office to assure it is properly posted.

My heart aches for you, but my lungs are reviving!

Believe me, I am your admirer as the...

Count von Hohenburg.

So, that accounts for Peleus, the remaining mystery from the Fold. He is now Janaczek, and he and Orestes are reunited. I folded the letter and placed it carefully in the box holding all the letters that followed, a candlestick box with a sliding lid converted for the purpose.

The letters are thrilling, I thought as I put them away. *But, what lies ahead? He can commandeer a warship for a year, and I am endlessly ironing underwear for another princess. All right, the new me is a countess, but once a princess always a princess, I say. That must be true everywhere but the Habsburg Empire where we are all marked at birth and fixed in ink on parchment as never-changing twigs to family trees by men—men who look at warm babies and can only draw cold lines of succession. I have a good job and live in a comfortable palace, but there is no sense of permanence for me here.*

The Vienna I was immersed in was alive with creativity and new thinking! Yet, the contrasts were so stark. On one hand, it was steeped in tradition and rich culture. At the same time, the city attracted innovative thinkers in psychology, music, and social protest bordering on mayhem.

I wondered what it would take to combine the societies of merit and aristocracy. *Hmm…perhaps me, with a certain free-spirited royal with a chronic cough.* At least I dreamed of it.

And what could have been more randomly accidental than the position of Franz Ferdinand as heir presumptive to the empire? Crown Prince Rudolph blasted that all away at Mayerling in a suicide pact with his mistress. *I cannot bear the thought of Franzi as a love-starved emperor suffering in silence and secret liaisons. We absolutely shall be a married couple! How difficult would that be?*

The candlestick box filled with more and more letters. In recent ones he disparaged mercilessly the attempts by mothers in Canada, Chicago, and New York to hurl their daughters at him. I almost felt sorry for the girls. *Almost.* But eventually my secret Count von Hohenburg and his companion, Janaczek, keeper of royal gardens, pheasants, and secrets, returned to Le Havre and eventually to Vienna. Princess Isabella's resolve had not waned in the meantime.

There were more hunting events and, of course, tennis at the Halbturn castle. We were doubles partners. There was a photo of us. I obtained an extra copy from which I clipped my image and put it in an expensive (for me) locket; I gave it to him with a kiss.

Isabella never stopped contriving important occasions in which she could re-hurl her timid Maria Christina at the next emperor. Isabella did not allow grass to grow under her tightly laced, high-ankle, dark brown calfskin shoes.

"This will do very well," she exclaimed to me one day as we poured over invitations for the early spring. "Count Heinrich Larisch von Moennich and Countess Henriette will hold a masked ball at the Larisch Palace in Vienna. I'll write our acceptances to Yetta. Do you dance well, Sophie?"

"Yes, and I love to."

"Kindly help Maria Christina learn the steps between now and then. And, in that case, you will go. We will all go. If it goes well there, I have my eye on one in Prague, later."

CHAPTER FIFTEEN

The first thing I taught Maria Christina was the intricate dance before the dance. It is the part that takes place in the vestibule and hallway leading to the ballroom. Before the first dance in the ballroom, all the boys form a line, and all the girls form another line. When the orchestra strikes up a march, the two lines march side by side through the center doors all the way to the orchestra stage, then separate and march to the rear of the ball room where they meet, bow and curtsey, then march as couples, arm in arm, to the stage again. The object of the dance before the dance is to spot the person you want to end up with and then jockey for position in the lines. There's never enough room in the vestibules and no one wants to create a commotion, so it is practice in stealth. It's bad form to change places once you've entered the ballroom, so you have to get it right out there, where it's dark, in the very beginning.

Early spring though it may have been, the night was cold with spits of icy rain. The ballroom of the Larisch Palace was alive with acres of candles and hothouse flowers. In the dimmer entry and vestibule, footmen were overtaxed having to move cloaks, capes, muffs, and woolen shawls to side and even upstairs rooms. Maria Christina, Isabella, and I arrived in the thick of it. Jostled and crowded, I did my best to scope the shape of the lines and decipher the wearers of the masks. After the introductions and greetings exchanged with our hosts, we put our heads together and started counting noses. I made Maria Cristina take a few turns and dips on the waxed parquet floor to make sure she had a feel for its sparse traction under cold, stockinged feet and slippers. For the occasion I had fashioned a long, dark-green skirt with wide pleats, covered by a rust-colored long apron falling nearly to the hem of the skirt. Over my white blouse I wore a red velvet long-sleeved waistcoat with wide lapels. I tied an azure silk sash around my waist with a bow with droopy loops. I dispensed with a mask so as not to be missed.

The Archduke arrived late but before the entrance march. Despite his elaborate disguise, no one believed that there was an actual Bohemian shepherd at the ball in bloused, yellow flaxen trousers tucked into high, brown leather boots, and a linen shirt under a pilled, brown woolen vest. Nor did anyone believe that the faux-shepherd's head was really that of a Carpathian wolf.

The game was on. Twice I had to reposition Maria Christina to align with the lone wolf's position. The drums rolled. The violins commenced. The lines began to move. At the ballroom doorway, the wolf-shepherd stepped aside and dropped one place back. Too late! We were inside. We marched to the front, returned, and rejoined the boys. They raised their left arms, and we rested our long-gloved hands atop our escort's arm. It was I who had the Archduke and Maria Christina who had a shambling gondolier. It couldn't be helped.

On the downbeat of each measure the couples looked at each other, and then turned their heads forward until the next downbeat.

"How's the tennis coming?" asked my wolf before we turned to take the next step, step, step.

"It's a long, boring game," I said, then turned and stepped, stepped, stepped.

"Doubles are best," he said. Step, step, step.

"Couples are better." Step, step, step.

"There are legal issues," he said flatly. Missed step, step, step.

Not knowing what to say to that, I made the final turn in silence. At the apron of the orchestra's stage, the dancers parted into single file lines and marched to the rear of the ballroom before rejoining.

"Issues that baffle an archduke?" I asked, and remained facing him through the next three steps.

"I'm trying to learn the rules," he said while still facing away.

"Archdukes have rules?" Stamp, stamp, stamp.

"Stifling ones. You wouldn't believe." Stumble, recover, step.

"I already don't. At least I don't want to hear them."

After the lines diverged and we reached the rear, I tugged at Maria Christina's elbow and slid ahead of her. I whispered, "Be sure to tell him clearly that you're *you* on the next pass, Maria Christina," I said. "Ignore him if he starts babbling about rules. I'm going to sit and have a think with a drink."

I did watch them, though. The wolf kept looking around for me through the rest of the march and afterwards. I moved from table to table. The wolf in shepherd's clothing kept following after me. We were a bit of a spectacle. Soon everyone was gossiping. I was having more fun at this than listening to his rules.

I MADE IT A habit to be near the tradesmen's door every morning and every evening around the same times. The familiar footman had learned this routine. One afternoon I had stood there long enough to know he wouldn't be coming with a letter. I had just turned away when I heard a knock.

He never knocks, I thought. I returned to see a figure in the shadows. I opened the door. It was Archduke Franz Ferdinand, dressed as his footman. He stood in jet black trousers and boots, an embroidered and buttoned vest the color of rich caramel, nearly hidden by raised embellishments of gold thread; and a white, straight collared shirt with matching straight bow tie. Over that, he wore a cutaway wool twill coat the color of camel's hair. It had seven tiers of elongated, gold embroidered, buttonhole decorations ending in burnished gold buttons, and three matching buttons from the cuff outside each of the long sleeves.

The uniform fit him perfectly. He was so smug he couldn't control his smile.

"We are not hiring," I informed him.

"I've been to Doctor Eisenmenger again. He confirms that I have tuberculosis."

I slumped against him. He held me. We were silent. I was near panic.

He spoke again, "As before, the remedy will be a voyage on the Mediterranean and to spread myself on Egyptian sands to dry out. But I didn't come here to complain. It is time for us both to meet with Sissi. I sense from what I hear at the palace that we need her wisdom."

"Palace gossip needs special palace wisdom to understand?"

"You ask me in that way, as if gossip always lacks gravitas and concern. Just come with me now for a secret rendezvous. She is looking forward to receiving us in her chambers."

I blushed and clutched at my hair. "I must change."

"No, Sophie. Never change. But to your point, come as you are. I mean, look at me. But, be careful to not display shock or surprise when you see how Sissi has changed. She is inhumanly thin. She stays on a permanent diet."

WHEN WE ARRIVED AT Hofburg Palace, the Swiss Gate was in shadows. Franzi and I stepped from the carriage and were joined by his real footman in matching livery. I entered the Swiss Gate between the arms of two footmen, both grinning like schoolboys, both of them flirting with me. Arm in arm we progressed two skips forward, half a step back. It was fun, my first for a long time. They wanted us to go for wine after. The long winter was at last over.

Empress Elisabeth's chambers were lit by overhead chandeliers and floor-to-ceiling windows on the outer wall, their massive, cedar-brown drapes tied back. The walls were nearly twenty feet high, painted the color of creamy buttermilk, highlighted with gold gilt over every archway, column detail, and door molding in the vast space. On a lush Persian carpet in the center of the room sat an iron single bed, bounded by a three-paneled vermillion folding screen. A rack holding fencing foils, a sport she took up in her late forties, adorned an interior wall. Above the bed dangled two gymnasium rings, suspended from the ornate ceiling by long leather straps.

Svelte and lovely, fifty-five-year-old Sissi reclined on the bed in a long, pearl-gray, iridescent gown of moiré silk. Without a word she sat up and reached for the rings. She pulled herself erect and propelled her legs with vigorous kips and swings until she was able to let go of the rings, clear the foot of the bed, and land on stockinged feet. She beamed in self-congratulation and came to embrace me.

Oh, the memories that greeted me, even with an exquisitely slight whiff of the sea. She was now nearly a foot taller, slender, with porcelain skin and very mortal, very blue eyes. She turned her face at an angle and conspicuously batted her long eyelashes. She held my hands as she stood back, her brows arched and slightly drawn with emotion.

"Whatever else you may have obtained in your bold leap," she declared, "you've been graced with an alluring, ample bosom. You may dismiss your footman." Franzi bent over, turned, and shuffled to the window, swallowing laughter. "You see, Sophie, that's the way you must disarm him every now and then."

After our laughter subsided, I said, "I have obtained much more, Your Highness, especially in recent weeks, and now in this reunion."

"Yes, I've been following it all. The signs point to your advantage."

"Do you foresee such?"

"No. Those days are behind me. I am as surprised as the next person by random or even secretly planned events."

I gripped her slender hands. "I am so sorry for your loss, Madam."

She inhaled deeply and sighed slowly. "Thank you. There have been so many. My firstborn with Franz Josef was also named Sophie; she died when two. I am truly jinxed in the male heir department. Rudolf was no hero with imperishable fame, but he was my only son, again, and tragically disturbed. In a misguided burst of gunpowder, he found release from inheriting rule of the empire. He tossed that to you, Franzi, like an imperial egg: cracked but not yet broken, for you to grip but not too hard, mind you. Yes, Sophie, my own heart cracks yet again. It is too much. I am more than sorry, dear Sophie. I am crushed. Emotionally, I mean, not paralyzed, of course. I am still spry and active.

"I travel to take my mind elsewhere. 'When I am in the hills, I want to be in the valleys, and when I sleep in the fields, I want to be on the sea.'"

Franzi turned and said, "That is truly beautiful, Your Highness. It is also beautifully true. I have felt the exact same yearnings for a place if I am in the wrong place."

Sissi said, "I do write poetry now, but that is not mine. I learned it traveling, of course. It is by a woman who lived in Croatia with a group of nomadic Romani, Gina Ranjicic. Despite her beautiful character and her poetic gifts, Gina's life and lot as a Romani brought her finally to crushing poverty. Franzi, yours will be a *dual* monarchy. The kingdom of Hungary has revered me for over thirty years as I galloped and jumped across its meadows, fields, and hillsides. Its people love me as I do them. Copies of my photograph have sold by the thousands there. They hang on walls of stately homes and shepherds' huts alike.

"Keep that in mind, Franzi, when you are the kaiser. Always protect the likes of Gina. Never forget and never underestimate the worth of Hungary and its people. My innermost soul reaches out in sympathy to the proud, steadfast people of that land. Do not fall into the snobbery so prevalent in the Austrian court."

Franzi did not reply but rather crossed his arms. I knew that he had decidedly different views on Hungarians but did not wish to contradict the Queen of Hungary.

Sissi continued, "For my remaining life and lot, I have my sights set on somewhere else. Come, let me show you."

She led us behind the paneled screen where a large tripod easel held a bundle of architectural drawings. "This is on Corfu. It is my retreat from the poisonous intrigues of this palace. I sail there on the *Miramar* whenever I'm able; you know me and sea voyages. Anyway, look at these renderings. I started it two years ago, right after we lost Rudolf. The sun and deepest blue skies and sea there simply must be experienced to understand. You know this of course, Franzi, better than anyone else. It will be my summer palace and filled with statues and tributes to swift-footed Achilles. I call it 'Achilleion.' In it I shall both forget and remember in equal measure as my years finally become final."

"It is perfect for you," I said.

She laughed, "On top of all that, there are dolphins everywhere. Now that we have found one another there is something I must say. You are here on matters of the heart. You want to marry."

"Yes," I said.

"Yes," said Franz.

"That will be somewhat less than perfect for the vipers crawling around this palace. Franzi, you will need the emperor's permission."

"Of course," he replied.

"It will be a heavy lift. You know the rules, do you not?"

"Someone close to me mentioned rules," I said. "But, no, I actually don't know what you mean."

"It is beyond ridiculous, Sophie," she said. "But in the eyes of the nitpickers, your blood, though handsomely blue, is not quite a dark enough shade of blue. Habsburg protocol is steeped in the exclusivity of those eligible to form a dynastic marriage. Royals may only marry into certain other royal families, hence the prevalence of fools ruling the continent. I could criticize it on and on, but there you are."

I was stunned. "So, it is all for nothing. It is impossible."

"No, my dear, I did not say *impossible*, I said 'a heavy lift.' Franzi, have you talked to your uncle about this?"

"No, Sissi, I have not done so yet. I do know what you're talking about. I had always assumed he would find a way through the legal issues. Sophie is a countess and her family have been loyal to our family since the Middle Ages. The emperor may be rigid, but I know him to respect true love. He holds such for you, as you know. I have not yet put the question exactly, but lately he has taken me more into his confidence and I am encouraged by that."

Sissi sighed and sank slowly against the edge of the bed. She shook her head. When she looked up, she said, "Never assume when it comes to fine points of law. Before thinking great thoughts, read the statute. It is codified in the 1839 House Law." She picked up a leather-bound book she had placed there for this occasion. "Here is a copy. You know all about me and books. Under it, your marriage would be considered morganatic, or left-handed, even assuming you've obtained the emperor's consent. If you marry without his consent, Franz Ferdinand will be stripped of all titles and entitlements. The best you should even hope for is his consent to the morganatic option."

She stood suddenly. She tapped her long finger against the other hand in emphasis. "Look, I want to help you. You may be right about my husband's sentimentality, but there is another salient point. He is, and thus you will be, emperor of the Dual Monarchy of this domain and Hungary, although after sixty years that cement has never completely dried. The Magyar Kingdom's dynastic law and custom have no royal marriage limitation like that of Austria. So, you and she could be King and Queen of Hungary, but not Emperor and Empress of our domain. Absurd. Don't let up on that; see if the nitpickers can talk themselves around the absurdity.

"Go to Franz Josef immediately and then let me know what he says. I will not leave Vienna until I have intervened with him on your behalf. I do have influence, although you'd never know it by appearances."

"But no one could possibly object," he said.

"Ah, again do not make assumptions. Even if the emperor is inclined to consent, and I believe he would be, his imperial chamberlain would be dead set against it. He is the keeper of customs and traditions around here. It is him you must satisfy."

"I barely know the man," Franz said.

"That will change, children, believe you me. The entire society of Vienna knows him as Count Alfred of Montenuovo. His father was chamberlain before him and gained your uncle's unquestioned trust. The father's health is failing. It's expected that on his death the son will be named Prince Alfred, Second Prince of Montenuovo, and he will become even more insufferable. Moreover, he married a Kinsky, so her father is related to your mother, Sophie; cousins, I suppose. I wouldn't count that as much advantage. Kinsky blood though she and you both may have, she is now distinctly a Montenuovo, and his influence is well baked in. There is no doubt that her loyalties would lie with him, not you."

Sissi then walked to me, her eyes soft. She clutched my shoulders. "But that's not the half of it, my child. You do know him very well, but not as Montenuovo. You last saw him on a galloping horse screaming profanities at you."

THE NEXT TIME THE real footman stood in the tradesmen's doorway of the Palais Albrecht, he was unsmiling. As he handed me two envelopes, I saw the black band on his upper arm. The envelopes were edged in thick, black ink with uncertain edges made by a trembling hand. I thanked him and went to my chambers and opened the one addressed to me. It was from Franz Ferdinand, and it told me that his father, Karl Ludwig, had died. I put the letter in the candle box and then hurried to Isabella's study.

She read her letter impassively. She looked at me and asked, "Do you have black attire in Vienna?"

"Yes, Madam," I said. After a pause, I said, "What is the occasion?"

Isabella looked at my face searchingly. She arched her eyebrows and said, "Must you ask?"

"Not if it makes you uncomfortable, Madam. I didn't mean to pry. I shall accompany you wherever you tell me to."

"Yes, you shall, but the funeral has no personal connection with you. Maria Christina and I must be strong for the heir to the throne, whose father has passed away. This entire household, including you, is officially in mourning. Cancel our diaries of any plans we may have made for the rest of May."

CHAPTER SIXTEEN

Habsburg aristocratic rankings nettled me even at my own father's funeral. I yearned to have Sophie at my side. Instead, I had Maria Theresa, my brothers Otto and Ferdinand Karl, and sister Margaretha, in the second pew, behind the emperor and Sissi.

Sophie stood at the rear of the cathedral. I learned that Isabella had instructed her not to sit with her and Maria Christina.

I had not witnessed such an elaborate and grand ceremony before. The music was Bach's church cantata, *Ich habe genug*, "I have enough."

After the service, the family and the pallbearers set off for the imperial crypt at the Capuchin church. In a ceremony centuries old, but never set out in a written document, the funeral party stopped at the closed door of the church. Montenuovo stepped to the front and banged his staff against the door.

From within came a voice, "Who seeks to enter?"

Montenuovo then thrust his chest out and recited Father's name and his four Austrian orders and decorations, followed by all thirty-five titles and honors bestowed by other nations. He was covered in medals and sashes.

From within, the voice said, "We know him not."

Montenuovo inhaled to respond, his face a picture of affected piety. I wouldn't have it! I stepped forward and gripped his forearm. I placed my forefinger to my lips to hush the lord chamberlain, who fell into a surprised silence. Then I repeated the ancient response, "A small, mortal man; a sinner." Whereupon, in keeping with tradition, the door swung open.

Sophie had followed us to the church. I turned and extended my hand to her. Sissi whispered something to the emperor. He turned to look at Sophie and brought his hand to his plumed hat in a two-fingered salute. After a moment's hesitation, she joined us at the door. Montenuovo fumed but said nothing.

Following Karl Ludwig's interment inside the cramped Tuscan vault, as everyone turned to leave, the emperor put his hand on mine to hold me back. In turn, I gripped Sophie's hand and held her back to stay with me. Montenuovo began to protest but the emperor instructed him to wait for him outside. Montenuovo glared at Sophie as he left.

We sat on prayer chairs, knees nearly touching, in the gloom of the candles. Emperor Franz Josef cleared his throat.

"Franzi, this is a good time for us to have a frank talk about succession."

Startled, Sophie made to leave, but I whispered, "Please stay."

The emperor acknowledged her with a warm smile, as would any gentleman of the court, but proceeded as if she weren't there to hear. He said, "I wish to talk about fitness to serve."

I shrugged and said, with a smile, "Your Highness, you seem in top form, and I see no reason you should not continue to serve."

There was a long silence. The emperor studied my face, which was passive until I gave him a slow wink and a twinkling smile. At that, the man arched his brows and began a rumbling guffaw. His face reddened. He held out his hand and I took it to steady him until he had finished laughing.

"Franz Ferdinand, I have not seen such cheeky humor in you before. You often appear humorless in public. Now, about fitness for service, I am, of course, referring to your own fragile health. You have us all worried about your tuberculosis, Sissi most of all. I mean no disrespect, but this is an occasion to look at facts as they are. I'm being urged in some quarters to consider Otto as sturdier stock for the next emperor."

I said, "Of course, Otto is both young and sturdy. But I am intimately aware of every aspect of my own health, Sire. I have breathed well at times and poorly at times throughout my life, in every climate in the world. I assess my strengths daily. I tell you confidently and humbly that I have never been so optimistic of my fitness to serve from a physical point of view. Doctor Eisenmenger is encouraged to believe I may be entirely rid of my disease in a matter of a year or so. As for Otto's youth, you must not hold that against him. Nevertheless, I do hold a greater maturity which has been much improved through my travels."

The emperor dipped his head in agreement. "You are diplomatic, Franzi. Otto is impetuous and has shown more interest in decadence than in matters of state. You, on the other hand, have developed a strong interest in the empire. You and I have disagreed about politics in the past, but that demonstrates the health of your independent will and soul. I'd like you to tell me how you see the future of the empire, and how you would govern."

I did not hesitate. I certainly did not need to "think on my feet" or scramble for an answer. I knew my mind and my answer.

"The empire is under the strain of the same nationalistic pressures building elsewhere in Europe," I began, but he broke in.

"Yes, yes, of course, that's been true for all of the fifty years I've ruled. I need to understand where you stand on the issue, where your heart is about preserving the pride and status of the empire."

I gathered myself. "Your Highness, I stand four-square fully committed to maintaining the pride and status of the empire. Dissolution of the empire would set the peoples of Europe against each other with such devastating enmity the result would be apocalyptic tragedy. Yet, the internal pressures, which as you say are so obvious, absolutely must not be ignored. Nationalism for each of the various populations of the Habsburg Empire would reduce the collective influence of those populations to that of a hutch of rabbits. We absolutely must maintain imperial readiness on land and sea to protect our people and lift them up over time. I vehemently oppose the nationalist tendencies of coffee-house rebels and poets. Yet, we cannot deny or contain the natural desires of people to be free of tyranny or perceived tyranny. The words of the American Declaration of Independence are more than a century old. That genie cannot be returned to its sealed jar."

The emperor scoffed, "Those were the words of revolutionaries. They must have been on the snarling lips of Maxmilian's executioners."

"They were words of the European Enlightenment before they were the words of colonial militias," I said. "Look what the Americans have achieved in the last hundred twenty-five years, Uncle. Theirs is the scheme of government that I say should be the future of the Dual Monarchy: a recognition of its diverse regions as 'states,' with overarching allegiance to the yellow and black flag of the House of Habsburg; a federal government of constituent states, the United States of Greater Austria. My vision of the empire matches that of Francis the Second's to unify the realm after Bonaparte's destructive adventures. But, the resulting rise in the autonomy of the Slavic people cannot mean reducing the status of Austrians. Necessarily, then, it must be at the expense of the Hungarians."

The crypt was silent for several minutes. Franz Josef finally said, "That is a lofty goal. The example of America is not quite apt, however. Yes, it achieved independence and then made itself into a federation of states. But that is the significant difference and points up the impracticality of your vision. In the United States of America, the constituent parts came together. In the case of the Habsburg monarchy, it would be an exercise of breakup and secession. That is a volatile and unpredictable pathway, dissociation instead of cohesion. Still, it is a worthy goal. It will take a lifetime. It will take patience."

Hearing that, I turned quickly to Sophie. I whispered to her, "Remember? It was foretold in your story: 'Innocence shall make... tyranny tremble at patience.'"

She gasped. "I had forgotten; yes, it makes so much sense."

I turned back to face my uncle. "Will you be seeking Otto's views on perpetuation of the empire?"

He said, "You are the deeper thinker, Franz Ferdinand. Otto is shallow and hedonistic. There is no need to ask his views on the subject; he has none to offer. Your vision is intelligent, vast, right, but messy. I'm glad I won't be here to see it."

I pressed him, "Majesty, will you—"

He waved his hand as if at a fly, "Put it in a letter? Not right now. You have to live by your words first, Franz Ferdinand. You speak eloquent words about preserving the empire." He turned to look unblinkingly straight at Sophie. "But, Franzi, you have to actually live by the rules, regulations, laws, and etiquette of the Austrian court." Turning back to me, he said, "Let me see you do that without wavering. When I do, then I'll dismiss randy Otto from my thoughts and give my blessings to you."

Sophie reddened. I gritted my teeth.

The air became close. The candles guttered. The emperor began to perspire, his breathing labored, a product of years of inertia. He was entrapped by those stifling years. I felt stronger than I had in a long time. I realized my life would be filled with the spirit-choking rules of a fossilized aristocracy. But I knew I would spend it with my Sophie.

It was time to go. I stood and said, "We should join the others. It's customary for there to be whiskey."

CHAPTER SEVENTEEN

There followed secret letters and surreptitious meetings, most of them at hunting lodges or on tennis courts. I became the Archduke's audacious tennis partner, a perfectly logical reason for him to ask for me whenever possible. This was a time of glorious days, stolen looks, and more treasured stolen kisses. I lived a love story and a spy story all at the same time. The combination produced narcotic moments of sensual elation on the one hand and edgy fearfulness of discovery and failure on the other. Where would it lead?

As fate would have it, it led to what felt like a fall from a mountain slope, as a climber might feel of a slipped grasp scaling a cliff. I got a bitter taste of the metaphorical medicine I had been forcing on Franzi, namely, "Your work is much less important than our romance and future family." That was too facile. Now I was about to feel the full weight of the importance of both love and work in a modern life.

I was an employed woman and grateful for the job. I may have bristled at the moods and vanity of my employer, but I never lost sight of the privileged fact that I was employed in work that provided a sumptuous place in which to live without want. For millions of single women approaching thirty in our world such a job—any job—would be worth a fortune. My job did entail menial tasks, but it provided occasions of luxury, travel, and excitement. I was a very lucky girl. At least I had work, and it was vastly more comfortable and stimulating work than that of millions of other unmarried women in cities and on farms. That employment was my real-life security and was nothing to trifle with. It bolstered my self-esteem.

Suddenly, I was fired from my job.

Franzi had clipped the locket with my photo to his large pocket watch along with other little items, such as a cigar clipper. We both thrilled at the secret knowledge of my visage always within his reach. Such a small pleasure. But, a small forgetfulness brought a typhoon of scandal and danger to our lives.

He left the watch, complete with fob, clipper, trinkets, and locket, in the men's dressing room at the tennis courts at Halbturn Castle. It was a mistake of haste which made waste. The maid who found it took it to Isabella. She recognized the watch immediately. She was puzzled over what might be within the locket. She thought she knew—a portrait of Maria Christina. How much more sensible it would have been for her to carry on with that thought, but that could only happen in fantasy. She, who had clawed open an imperial thank you note, unable to wait to use a letter opener, broke all bounds of privacy and opened the locket. Imagine her disappointment to see my smiling face.

"You ingrate! You deceitful country mouse of a criminal!" she raged. "All those tennis games were just to steal my daughter's future for yourself! You have no place in this household. Leave us and send me your resignation."

I was nearly blinded by the shock. At first, I forgot to breathe. Then, it hurt my heart to breathe. I stammered, "No! You are so very wrong."

"Do not ever contradict your betters, missy. I will inform the entire society of Vienna that you are the pickpocket of my daughter's heart."

She ranted for all in the household to hear. She then turned her vitriol to ruining my name in Vienna's aristocracy.

I left abruptly and went to stay with Zdenka in Vienna. She had rooms in the vast home of Stephanie, the widow of sad Rudolf, where Zennie worked as lady-in-waiting. It was there I finally wrote the resignation letter which Isabella had demanded.

FRANZI LOOKED DRAINED WHEN he came there to see me. Stephanie's household had just finished breakfast. The maids were raising dust and rolling carpets in their morning routine. Franzi had just been to Schonbrunn. He was pale, not only because his meeting with the emperor was before dawn, but also from what had transpired there. We sat in a corner of the great hall, rattling teacups, and spilling crumbs.

"Isabella had already been to see him," he said. "She filled his ear with distortions about my intentions toward Maria Christina. She had told him that I had been deceitful in leading her on just to carry on a clandestine affair with you. She had demanded that the emperor rebuke me in public and demanded that I make a formal apology to her and her daughter."

I broke in, "But Maria Christina was always clear-eyed about her prospects. She enjoyed the attention, but she had no expectations that you would marry her."

"I'm sure that's the case but the air had been completely poisoned before I got there. The emperor sort of waffled around about it and said it would be best for me to 'end the affair.' That was intolerable. I told him in direct language that this is no affair. I told him I had consulted Sissi and Maria Theresa about my love for you. I told him I had meant to put before him a formal request for his permission for us to marry, and that my stupidity in leaving the pocket watch behind had simply hastened the necessity for me to do so."

I thought, *truly stupid,* but held that thought. I said flatly, "What's done is done."

He stood and began to pace. "Be that as it may, the emperor sent for Montenuovo to come in. It didn't take long to find him; I believe the man lurks near the emperor's chambers to spy and then jump in whenever he has a chance. The emperor explained that I wanted to marry you. Montenuovo became brutal. You'd have thought I had wanted to have the emperor excommunicated or worse. He brought down all the arch condescension that he could muster. He declared that it was simply impossible."

I stood and grabbed his arm. "Franzi, let us leave! There are trains and passenger ships that could take us anywhere in a matter of hours. You must see now that you can't have it both ways, Franzi. A new world is open to us. You are not so invested in the Habsburg dynasty that you have to put up with all this. You literally fell into it!"

He stiffened, his brows pinched. "There has to be a way to reconcile this. I can't do this alone. We both have to find a better way than running away. There are no more edges left. We will have babies, I assure you."

I was filled with admiration and love at the same time. I said, "I'll hold you to that—the part about the babies." He laughed. "But what do we do next?" I asked.

He had already been thinking. "The art of governing is the art of diplomacy. The art of diplomacy is the art of alliance and compromise. First, we enlist people of influence who can help change the emperor's mind. Next, we try to reduce the influence of Montenuovo."

I said, "I'm without a job, Franzi. I have plenty of time. Put me to work. I could speak to Sissi again. She wants a report on your meeting—let me go to her. I can also muster support from the Chotek side of the family. Maria Pia's husband is a high-ranking archduke. What other allies?"

He said, "Sophie, we need the support of the pope."

"I have no pathway there. Since he's new, he'll likely be looking for your support as well."

"Perhaps he has a liberal mind," said Franzi. "I will ask Mama. Maria Theresa is an Infanta of Portugal. Her forebears helped the Church expand as her country gathered colonies. She can speak to Rome."

CHAPTER EIGHTEEN

Hermione, my storybook mother, I knew only by her beautiful name. I have been extremely fortunate to have had two other mothers in my life. First, there was Thetis, then there was Wilhelmine. She was a Kinsky. Close as I was to her, I did not know my Kinsky relatives very well at all. Soon, that would change.

Franzi had a terrible storybook mother and never really knew his Habsburg one. But he drew the top prize in the case of his stepmother. She was the most beautiful woman I had ever seen, for whatever that matters, and genuinely loved Franzi and his younger brothers and sister. The thing is, she never stopped clucking over them. She would fuss over Franzi as an adult as much as she did when he was eight. I suppose that's not so bad, considering the other extreme.

We did take our predicament to her. We made a visit to her baroque palace in Vienna. She was very practical about our situation, and very insistent about helping. She promised to organize letters to the pope and meetings between herself and Sissi for a campaign to press the case with the emperor.

Before we left, she pulled me aside. "Sophie, I want to make sure you know how you are connected to Count Montenuovo."

My eyes widened. I was struck dumb. *How could she possibly know that?* I wondered. But she wasn't talking about the escape from the Fold.

She said, "Your mother comes from the Kinsky family. Count Montenuovo married a Kinsky: Countess Franziska. There has always been a cloud of suspicion about Montenuovo, but I have no idea of what that is. It may be something you should look into. Perhaps there are chinks in Montenuovo's armor. You could use anything like that to help your case."

I was relieved, but certainly curious. "Where should I begin?" I asked.

"I wish I could be of more help, dear," she said. "I don't know much about the Kinskys. I never delved into Habsburg history; it was too dreary for me. I prefer the riper lifestyle of Portugal, its Fado and heavy lunches. I suggest you dig into it to find out your-self." This news was intriguing. We left Maria Theresa on a rather more positive note. She not only agreed to intervene in our favor, she offered to host our wedding at her Reichstadt castle, north of Prague. She even promised to put her own wedding veil on me!

I went back to where I was living temporarily with Zdenka. Since she was a lady-in-waiting there, I couldn't just take root in her household. I decided to leave, but where would I go? I chose to impose on various Kinsky families, in search of the elusive "cloud of suspicion" about Montenuovo. I was on trains to Grosspriessen, Moravia, Silesia, Salzberg, barely unpacking my bags from place to place. Finally, it was to Bohemia, where Ursala Kinsky, a cousin, lived alone.

Oh my! She knew a lot about the Count of Montenuovo. Her arthritic hand shook when she poured sherry in the tactile, cut-glass stemware. After she had settled most of her cats, she opened my eyes with what she knew.

"Montenuovo is opposed to your marriage, left-handed or otherwise. I know this from Franziska herself. I have her letter—somewhere. But I'll give you the gist. To Count Montenuovo, you are simply unsuitable, Kinsky and Chotek be damned. You are tainted because you are 'lesser' than Franzi. It would not only be against the rules but against nature itself. The count has pronounced it this way: 'She's not one of us.'"

"Ursala! That's as though I belong in a zoo."

"Indeed it is," she replied. "But hold on a moment. Put this in your bonnet. Montenuovo's own blood is thinner than he cares to admit. His father was illegitimate. In fact, his father's parents were not only unmarried when he was born but they were of unequal rank. You see, she was a bloody Habsburg! Another sherry, dear?"

"No," I said, breathlessly, trying to absorb these revelations.

"I think I'll have another, Sophie."

"Please tell me more, Ursala," I said, pressing my fingernails against the heels of my hands.

"Right," she said with a pinched smile. "Montenuovo senior arrived in the world by a dalliance between one Count Neipperg and the wife at the time of one *Napoleon Bonaparte*. The Little Corporal was blissfully unaware that he was being made even smaller while he was exiled on the island of St. Helena.

"When she became a widow, she finally married Neipperg, but it had to be the left-handed kind because she was a haughty Habsburg! Hilarious, don't you agree?"

"I do," I said, but wasn't laughing.

"Montenuovo's father was forever hoisted on the morganatic petard and could not even advance from count to prince until his Habsburg wife had died."

So, I thought, *that would warp Montenuovo's thinking before even considering his former desire, as Florizel, for me and his blind rage toward the man I chose over him.*

Armed with Ursala's information, I would confront the emperor myself. I'd look him in the eyes and tell him what his imperial court chamberlain was really all about. And if that didn't work, I was even prepared to explain to the kaiser all about the Fold!

WHEN I FINALLY ARRIVED back in Vienna, Franzi told me of his struggles. The most bitterly disappointing opposition was that of his brother, Otto, and his other brother, Ferdinand Karl. At that point it seemed hopeless. Franzi did gain an important ally. He insisted to all that the barrier to our marriage boiled down to a legal quirk. He turned to a man who had once tutored him in law, Max von Beck.

Beck traveled in the political and diplomatic circles of Vienna. He dealt in the everyday sausage-making drudgery of administering civil law. Franzi and Beck churned lawyers, politicians, and amateur court parasites over the intricacies and absurdities of an outmoded law in modern life.

Beck and Franzi organized a hunting party to which the prime ministers of Austria and Hungary would be invited. The Dual Monarchy's executive powers under the emperor were divided between them. In the cozy afterglow of a sumptuous meal, Beck and Franzi would seek their support. It was no mere accident that

Franzi chose Mayerling for the occasion. He wanted the stark proximity of Rudolf's tragedy to be the stage for their conversation. It would remind all of Crown Prince Rudolph's split life between a rule-conforming wife and the woman he loved.

Prince Franz Anton, the Austrian prime minister, came to the hunt still in his dark cutaway with gold epaulets. Kálmán Széll, prime minister of Hungary, showed up in a long suit jacket and tie, and a stiff white collared shirt. Neither man was an outdoorsman.

The hunt for hazel grouse, quail, and pheasant took less than an hour before the prime ministers were fatigued. Back at the lodge, Franzi challenged them with this question: How could you defend with a straight face a position that the Queen of Hungary is unsuitable as Empress of Austria?

Their retort was: Franzi could avoid the absurdity by agreeing that his wife would be neither Queen of Hungary nor Empress of Austria. In other words, both positions were equally absurd from the political and legal points of view.

It all resembled a French farce, with maids, archduchesses, constitutional lawyers, and churchmen whirling in and out from doors opening and slamming shut. Clearly it would take more than that to win the emperor. Franzi and I would have to face the emperor ourselves and have it out with him.

But a dark interval suddenly paused the farce. There was news of a tragedy.

CHAPTER NINETEEN

Sophie was a puddle of grief and tears. She told me that she could only properly grieve for Thetis in a meadow on a warm, autumn afternoon.

Thetis's days—millennia, really—of unorthodox adventures and tortured memories ended in September, suddenly, on a street in Geneva. She was stabbed in the heart by an anarchist who couldn't find his original victim (the visiting Duke of Orleans) and turned on Sissi as an opportunistic secondary target. I grew cold at the thought that death by murder must be a Hapsburg genetic trait.

Sissi's final words were, "At last." For Sophie and me, the death of Thetis called for joy for her long-sought victory over the pain of a mother's loss.

Janaczek led a small party of us to a meadow a few hours' walk from a rural train stop between Prague and Vienna. I wore a tunic—no, not the one trimmed in purple. This tunic was white linen with broad sleeves and tucked into loose, black trousers bloused below the knees in the Hungarian style, in deference to Sissi. Sophie wore a leaf-green dirndl with lavender top from her girlhood.

Zdenka was also there. Zennie was the only person in the empire to whom Sophie confided her earliest memories of the Thetis we knew and loved before she was Sissi. Zennie refused to believe a word of it, convinced that Sophie had hallucinated. Sophie concluded that Zennie could never tell it to anyone. As a result, Zennie knew that this day would be profoundly unofficial and involve tributes that would seem pagan in content. She would take that in good humor, even as a devout Catholic and an unshakably confident believer.

Janaczek was stalwart in keeping a level temperament. He threw himself into the task as bearer of the few things we took with us, a labor into which he could invest his own deep feelings.

From a slope at one end of the meadow a spring rises with a strong, burbling flow which then flattens in a bog before rushing away at the other end and eventually to the Danube. In dappled sunlight, Janaczek unrolled the architectural drawings of the Achilleion beside the spring and propped them on the moss with fern fronds that had turned brown at the finish of summer. He placed a clump of sheep's wool next to the Achilleion.

I kneeled on the moss and poured out a small flask of lingonberry wine. Sophie placed next to that a small bouquet of rosemary and red poppies. She recited a poem written by Sissi herself:

"O'er thee, like thine own sea birds
I'll circle without rest
For me earth holds no corner
To build a lasting nest."

I had committed to memory a section of Alexander Pope's translation of the *Iliad*. Still flummoxed by the English tongue, I recited these couplets, in which Thetis cries to her Nereid sisters over Achilles' grief on the death of Patroclus:

"Hear me, and judge, ye sisters of the main!
How just a cause has Thetis to complain!
How wretched, were I mortal, were my fate!
How more than wretched in the immortal state!
Sprung from my bed a godlike hero came,
The bravest far that ever bore the name.
Like some fair olive, by my careful hand
He grew, he flourish'd and adorn'd the land.
To Troy I sent him: but the fates ordain
He never, never must return again.
So short a space the light of heaven to view,
So short, alas! and fill'd with anguish too!
Hear how his sorrows echo through the shore!
I cannot ease them, but I must deplore.
I go at least to bear a tender part,
And mourn my loved-one with a mother's heart."

Janaczek drew the hurdy-gurdy strapped over his back around against his belt buckle. He turned the small crank at the end of its lute-shaped body. On the keyboard at the neck, he played as Sophie danced a courtly French sarabande. He followed this with a lusty Hungarian czardas, slow at first but with a wild finish that was too quick for even for her feet!

Zdenka clapped. Although she did not know Elizabeth in the same way the others of us had, Zennie is a solemn and empathetic woman. She brought as her offering a haunting chant in Latin composed in medieval Germany by Hildegard of Bingen. When she finished, she stepped to me.

"Archduke, my song was for the empress. Now, may I offer to you some wisdom from the writings of the very same Abbess Hildegard? From what I know of you through my sister, you may find her visions to be supportive of yours. I render her original to modern vernacular as this: 'We cannot live in a world interpreted for us by others. An interpreted world lacks hope. To conquest terror is to take back our listening, to use our own voice, and to see our own light.'"

I nodded and said, "I shall welcome the day I may address you as my sister-in-law."

Zennie smiled. "Archduke, I welcome it as well. You are not as gruff as people say!"

BACK IN VIENNA, THE service for Sissi was somber and impersonal. The emperor sat alone at the front. I sat with my brothers and sister in the pew behind him. Sophie, of course, was required to sit in the vast, inconspicuous middle of the cathedral. Afterward, we stood before the doors of the Capuchin church. Again, the doors opened after the ritual knocks, calls, and responses. Again, I gripped Sophie's hand as we entered, to the chagrin of the imperial chamberlain. The air was stuffy in the echo-chamber that was the new, anticipatorily named Franz Josef vault. This time, it was I who tugged the emperor's sleeve to stay behind.

"Uncle, I want to speak of fitness to serve," I stated. The emperor looked around with lifted eyebrows but said nothing.

"I want to speak to you about fitness of my mind as I desire it to be, should it fall to me to rule the empire. I need to speak to you about my sense of self. For over thirty of your fifty years of reign, you had the love and intimacy of the one we just laid to rest, Europe's most accomplished woman. Your love for her was genuine. So, too, is my love for Sophie. I ask you here and now to bless my choice of wife. It is Sophie. There has been scandalous gossip about her character and mine as well. We will satisfy any question you may have by our own sworn explanations to you. We do not want you to have any lingering doubts about our good faith."

Franz Josef fidgeted and said, "Franzi, old boy, look here, you have a steady and discerning eye when it comes to women. You have turned down countless opportunities to marry within the strictures of Habsburg protocol. I might have felt the same in your shoes. Sophie is a gem. While I admire the wisdom of your choice, I cannot grant you the power to change the royal protocol. Just do as all the others have: marry a royal and keep a mistress. It is the compromise of kings."

I stood. "Why should I want such a life? You would have me as another royal hypocrite? You would cut me along a centerfold into two halves and remake me with a private self and an imperial self? A double life is no life at all! I couldn't live with myself that way anymore than your son, Rudolph, could. You would have me disown the one love of my life. I intend to pledge and honor my marriage vows, just as you have done. Why should I be relegated to a life of deception and infidelity?"

"Because it's the done thing!" snorted the emperor. "I can't compromise the law. Shall we get Montenuovo in here to explain it? He's probably just on the street, beside himself."

I struggled to remain calm. I said, "Compromise is a principle of statecraft, not of self, not of love."

Then Sophie spoke up. "Sire, I have spent a great deal of time looking into your chamberlain, Count Montenuovo. What I've discovered is very revealing. It will shock you. His own father was a bastard, conceived and birthed out of wedlock by another man's wife. That woman, as a Habsburg, outranked the man in aristocracy. I think those facts explain why he is opposed to us. He lives in his family's hidden shame and thus expects us to as well. I do hope this sheds some light on this whole question."

The emperor scraped his chair to face her. "Sophie, you do not think that you have uncovered some deep, dark secret, do you? Of course, I know about Montenuovo; how could I not? It was bloody Bonaparte that his grandfather made cuckold! It may not be public knowledge, but we Habsburgs know it very well. I'm sorry you wasted your time on this. You could have simply asked me."

Her face seemed to freeze. Still, she persisted. "Don't you see? The point is not the surprise, it is the significance. If you've known of it, how could you not know its significance? His personal history has deeply affected him psychologically."

He stood and fumed, "'Psychology!' There's a word I detest. A handful of savants use Vienna as a coven for this new cult! It is sacrilegious! It is babble! Psyche me no psychology, please, or I'll—"

"Uncle," I interrupted, "Just listen to what she means. The simple fact is that this dynastic law is out of date. The father of your chamberlain was in its straitjacket. Both of them have been bent under the weight of it all their lives. Two generations of your very own chamberlains have been too conflicted to advise you with clear, unbiased judgment. That's why Montenuovo brooks no breach of the old rule. He is vested in its permanence. Just because he elevates the law beyond its usefulness, you don't need to. Let it fall into the disuse it deserves and then repeal it."

The emperor rolled his eyes and thumped his open palm against his chest. "Enough, Franz Ferdinand!" His shout reverberated in the vault. *"Do you want to wear this sash edged in purple or do you not?"*

With that, I crowded close to his face, on the verge of losing all composure. "I am no stranger to purple trim, Uncle!"

We glared at each other. Eventually the emperor blinked and returned to his seat. He turned to Sophie and said, "Don't think me a brute. None of this is personal, my girl, I hope you understand."

"Sire," she uttered in a furious burst, "I don't believe it! No, I am sorry, but I do not understand. Perhaps I should just leave so as to not take up so much royal oxygen."

I broke in, "Uncle, you said that you are unable to compromise the law. But surely there is compromise somewhere. Rather than stand at the edge of the irreconcilable, let us look for a middle way."

The emperor grumbled, "Franzi, you are stepping out onto dangerous ice. The only middle way would cost you dearly. If I were to consent to a morganatic marriage—and that's a big 'if'— your wife and your children could not inherit the throne from you."

"Not if you were to make reasonable exceptions," I said, hoping for compromise, again.

"Emperors make no exceptions, Franzi! You'd better get used to that fact."

"I am going to marry Sophie Chotek, Uncle! You'd better get used to that one."

"You might just take a more conciliatory tone with the man who holds the fate of you, your wife, and your heirs in his hands. Show me your own spirit of compromise."

Sophie whispered to me, "Think about uncrowned babies, Archduke. Babies dependent upon our love and care and who never desire for more than that from you and me."

She was right to bring me back to essentials. I relaxed my shoulders. I smiled. "Of course, you are right, Uncle. Compromise assures getting that which is most valued, no matter the cost. I will renounce the rights of my surviving wife and children to claim the throne of the Habsburg Empire after my death. Having done so, will you grant your permission for us to marry and for me to fulfill my destiny to rule this domain?"

"You drive a hard bargain, Franzi. In a vault with my name on it, you twist my old arm after I lost the love of my life. I repeat, I'm not a brute. I know the force of love. Yes, I suppose I can live with that. You'll have to do it in public and in writing. More importantly, as I said before, you have to live your oath to Habsburg court rules. Now, may we join the others? It's customary for there to be whiskey."

CHAPTER TWENTY

Just as my uncle had demanded, I made a public declaration and signed a document that said neither Sophie nor any of our children could ever succeed to the throne. With the stroke of the pen, I alone could rise to that position in our family. Sophie had assured me, "That is absolutely fine with me—now there will be a family!"

I have to say that it was a heavy sacrifice for me to renounce the rights of my unborn children. I had abandoned my progeny in that way when I fled Mycenae, and now I had done it again. Nevertheless, the momentous compromise was signed and sealed. But, would it be fulfilled?

By that I mean, would that transaction lead to a happy life? After all, the words of the renunciation would not spring into effect until my death, and I was just thirty-six years old. We anticipated a long life ahead of us, with me absorbed in governing fifty million people. What would that do to our marriage? The victory and true success would depend on how well we lived our lives. Yes, we had won the right to marry, but that would be only the beginning.

And what a beginning! Montenuovo immediately attacked Sophie personally. He always professed to be maintaining protocol and the norms of court customs, but his focus was always to insult her.

Those wounds came right on our July 2, 1900, wedding day. It wasn't in Vienna, it was at Reichstadt, as Maria Theresa had promised. Except for her and her two daughters, no one else in my family even attended the wedding. Montenuovo had concocted a conflicting two weeks of official mourning for the court because an obscure German princess had died in June.

Even Sophie's brother, Wolfgang, stayed away, worried that attending might reflect badly on him in the army. That speaks volumes about the gossip campaign against us, and more volumes about Wolfgang.

Sophie wore everything white: satin gown, chiffon flounces and lace, and Maria Theresa's antique veil that flowed into a seven-foot train. She had her hair up in braids with orange blossoms. Emperor Franz Josef made a nice gesture with the gift of a diamond tiara which she wore with pride. The hour and a half ceremony was over at noon. After luncheon of venison and champagne-slurred speeches, we sang the national anthem. The only other sign of anything imperial at the small ceremony was the telegram from the emperor's foreign minister announcing Sophie's elevation to Princess of Hohenberg, to be addressed as "Your Grace."

Truly, it was the most beautiful day of our lives. It was beyond the pinched imaginings as road mapped by our original storytellers. Still elated, I wrote to Maria Theresa a week later:

We are both unspeakably happy and this happiness we owe above all to you. Where would we be today if you had not taken our part in such noble and moving fashion! We can

*offer nothing in return but the assurance that you have done
a truly good work and have made your two children happy
for the rest of their days.*

*Soph is not reading this as she is busy just now sorting out
begging letters. That means I can tell you, just between our
two selves, dearest Mama, that Soph is a treasure and that I
cannot describe my happiness. She looks after me so well, I'm
doing famously, much less nervous and feeling so healthy. It is
as though I have been born anew. She is always singing your
praises and talks only of your goodness and your love....*

With the singular exception of Mama, my Habsburg family
were not exemplars of happy domestic life. My father had been
distant and morose. My brothers practically disowned me when
we announced our engagement. Otto wasted his life on hedonism,
and he died young because of it. I had few close friends other
than the lawyer, Beck, and Janaczek. It was my love for Sophie
that kept my head above the polluted waters of Schonbrunn and
its tribal aristocracy. Montenuovo was the tribal shaman in what
befell us at Belvedere Palace.

CHAPTER TWENTY-ONE

ontenuovo did nothing to directly offend Franzi; that
would have taken more courage and entailed greater risk to
his position than he was willing to venture. But that simply made
more conspicuous the offenses which fell on me almost daily.

For one thing, Franzi and I were not allowed to sit together
in the imperial box at a theater or concert nor he to sit anywhere
else but there. This was especially painful when we attended, sitting separately, a performance at the Imperial Opera House of the
newest Ricard Strauss opera, *Elektra*. I often glanced to the imperial box to observe how my husband was digesting the disturbing,
dissonant music, so different from his newest favorite, *The Merry
Widow*. He was absorbed in the lyrics. At one point Elektra sings,
in an anguished aria, the words, "Now I am truly alone." At this,
Franzi was visibly disturbed. He looked around for me. I caught
his eye. He was transfixed. I wanted to embrace him, but I couldn't.
It was heartbreaking. I, too, felt horribly alone. I didn't care where
I sat, but I cared deeply that Franzi was not at my side. This opera,
with its scorching scenes of despair and pathos, brought to life
onstage the mythical past of Orestes. It did not belong in our real
lives. I determined then and there to be a better woman in his life

than any of the defeated women onstage. Since I needed to be a wife above all, I needed to shut out the nonsense of Montenuovo. It was easier said than done.

We couldn't even ride together in the same carriage to the theater or anywhere else in Vienna. You see, the imperial coaches and carriages had narrow bands of gold gilt on the wheels and spokes. I was undeserving of the imperial wheels. I always had to go in a separate one with plain black ones. Ridiculous.

I COULD NOT BEAR the feeling that my self-worth had sprung a leak. I needed a friend. But I had that and more: I had a sister. I could always confide in Zdenka.

In her modest bedroom, and with Stephanie away for a few days for a saltwater spa, I poured out my heart. I said, "It got worse after that and even more personally humiliating. Let's say there was to be an official state dinner to honor some visiting dignitary. Depending on the rank of the dignitary, Montenuovo insisted that I could not even attend. Even that wasn't enough. Montenuovo always arranged for an empty chair next to Franzi with a full place setting. It would remain vacant throughout the affair. Franzi was infuriated. Each such occasion was a victory for Montenuovo. There was always some new twist of the knife in me."

Zennie said, "So, it's true then. I've heard such things rumored about when I listen in on Stephanie's confidential conversations."

"You still do that?" I asked with a smile.

"Old habits die hard," she said with a twinkle. "Go on."

"There was a dinner one time at Belvedere," I said. "Not of the kind from which I was banished, but I could not be seated next to Franzi. On this occasion my sleeve brushed a wineglass and it fell to the floor in a smash. Montenuovo himself stood, walked to me, and gathered the stem and unbroken part of the glass. He then placed the glass and shards in a heap of crystal splinters back on the table at the tip of the dinner knife. That was too much for Franzi. By the time Montenuovo was finished with his display, Franzi's footman had removed Montenuovo's chair altogether. Franzi broke the tittering by standing and declaring it was time for the men to move to the parlor for port and cigars."

Zennie stood and began to pace. "This is becoming intolerable. Why don't you say something to your husband? After all, as heir presumptive I would think he'd outrank Montenuovo."

"Zennie, I don't want to appear to be daunted by Montenuovo. If I permitted myself to display the true effect it has on me it would crush Franzi."

"He could do with a good crushing, sister!"

"No! I am more sensitive to the effect of Montenuovo's cruelty on Franzi than on me. He's devastated by it; depressed at times. He goes off with Janaczek for days at a time doing I know not what. I feel that I am the one at fault, Zennie."

"Bosh!"

"Of course, that is wrong to believe."

"Absolutely right: *wrong*."

"Yet in my situation it's inevitable to do so."

She said, "You are overthinking things. You're puncturing yourself with unearned guilt."

"Look," I said, "I don't doubt your point, but my point is that inside my mind I have caused unnecessary complications for him in the imperial government. Whenever Montenuovo lands one of his wounding blows on me, I do the only thing I can do which is to gracefully accept the slights and humiliation just as naturally as a summer cold."

"You can't mean that it is as simple as that for you," she said. "You must have stronger feelings about it than that. Tell me."

I didn't want to tell her. But, with tears on my twisted face I said, "I most certainly do, Zennie. I feel—*wrath!*

"You are not a wrathful person. I know you."

"That was then. But wrath is now my secret other sister, Zennie!"

FOR MONTHS AND MONTHS, I managed to maintain good humor, stifle the hurt, and appear sanguine about such things. At home I never complained about it to Franzi.

Then came the last straw to crack my calm. It was at one of the Belvedere banquets held during the visit of the Shah of Persia.

That evening is *seared* in my memory. I relive each moment in my mind even today.

I was permitted to attend, and even Zennie was to be there. Stephanie would be the guest of honor's dinner companion and Zennie would sit on her other side.

I was in the rear hallway with everyone else awaiting the grand entry to the dining room. But I was on my own, literally. Montenuovo placed Isabella on one side of Franzi and Maria Christina on the other. All the guests entered through massive double doors flung wide open to accommodate the transit of hooped gowns in a procession prescribed by rank. I waited as the last in line. When I approached the doorway, a footman slammed one door shut. I stood frozen at the opening, unable to proceed with decorum. No escort awaited my arrival to lead me to my place at the table. In shame, I turned away and stamped back to our chambers, face stinging with humiliation that my very own sister had witnessed my shame.

I WAS FURIOUS. OUR bedroom chambers at Belvedere had a small balcony overlooking the manicured French garden shaded by chestnut and fir trees. The gibbous moon rose late that night, very nearly midnight. I had thrown open the doors to the balcony. Of course, the air was cold. I didn't care. I was very hot, and I found the chill air cleansing. That was exactly what I thought our bedroom needed that night, a clearing of the air.

It took Franzi forever but eventually he did come in.

"Sorry, Soph, I lost track of the time," he muttered.

"That happens to you a lot, doesn't it?"

"Sophie, I'm not sure what you mean but I certainly understand why you would be upset."

"What I mean is, you often lose track of time and a lot of other things. Let's start with, for example, your inseparable *xiphos*. You lost that at least two times by my count. Then there was the time you lost time itself. You forgot your very own pocket watch! It's a good thing you had military aides with you who could get you on the train to Vienna. So dreary for you to lose the intimacy of that pocket watch, oh yes, and my photo along with it. You lost your watch, and I lost my job! I lost my reputation. I lost my livelihood, and what little esteem I had in society. But history will remember the only thing lost on that day of tennis was your shiny pocket watch—'bumbling, careless, loveable old Franzi, isn't he a stich?'"

"I know you're upset," he said calmly, "But why bring all that up tonight?"

"Because, Archduke," I was shouting now, "Since everything else is all about you, you need to face up to a few shortcomings. If you know why I'm upset, as you say, kindly tell me why you think I am."

"That Montenuovo—" he began.

"*No!* I'm not talking about a chamberlain, I'm talking about his superior, the Archduke! How does a chamberlain humiliate an archduke's wife and he remain passive? I remember when you punched him in the nose in front of a crowd of county folk. Where is that part of you now that we are a bit more up in the world?"

"Sophie, I have to walk a tightrope. Sometimes I can't always follow my instincts or impulses as a husband because of my life at court—"

"That says it all," I spat.

"—The day might come when I'll have to choose between being a Habsburg and being a husband, but it is not today. It was not in the ballroom when Montenuovo insulted you again. And it is not now, in the small hours. Let me explain—"

"*Explain* means 'talk.' I'm talking about action. *What are you going to do, Franzi?*"

"I am going to finish my sentences no matter how late we need to stay up. Sophie, duality is forged in my very nature: prince, then vagabond; soldier, then huntsman; shepherd, then avenger. Nature itself is forged that way. A hundred years ago, men of science made a discovery about light that has bewildered scholars to this day. When a beam of light was shone against a double-slitted plate, just like the Other Edge, it passed through as a wave, not as particles as had been believed. There is still an uncertainty whether its natural state is the one or the other. But, even if we lack certainty about the invisible, we are still agents of choice to some degree. I am an archduke through no choice of my own, but my life as Archduke is defined by what I choose to do with it.

"I can't help what fate might have in store for me. I only want to live according to my own good choices. I don't know how you and I gained second chances and new lives, but our lives are entangled with conflicting responsibilities.

"You heard Sissi exhort me to lift up the Hungarian half of the Dual Monarchy. Then you heard my uncle exhort me to preserve the primacy of the Austrian half. Dualities at odds. You also heard him declare that I was provisional depending on my fidelity to Austrian court protocol. It's truly a tightrope."

He was sitting on a bench at the foot of our bed. I began to pace in front of him. "You are remarkably nimble in walking a tightrope of high-minded ideas. I have simpler needs. All I'm asking for is to enter my own dining room freely and to take dinner with my own husband. But I see now that desire would impede your path to power."

"Does greed for power dominate me? No, but freedom and duty do. Those repelling dualities consume me. I told you once before, it would be greedy of me to exchange my responsibility to the peace of the realm for lighter duties. I had a responsibility to my Mycenean family, and I did my duty. But I found my way out of the muck. I found a way back to you.

"Of course I have to find a solution to Montenuovo's intolerable animus. I cannot discipline or dismiss Montenuovo. I could plead the case to Franz Joseph and beg him to take some action.

But, putting this matter at his disposal would be a risky ultimatum, Sophie."

I stopped pacing and pointed my finger at him. "Again, it's your oratory. I'm talking about deeds. Actually, I'm pleading! What will be your action? *What will you do, Franzi?*"

He rose and went to the balcony doors, shut, and locked them. The sun had just risen. "Please get dressed, Sophie. Dress for a journey."

"We are both exhausted, can't it wait?"

"No, Sophie. You have called for action. The fact of the matter is that I have already acted. Now it is time for you to see what it is. I need to go organize our movements and send telegrams. We leave just as soon as you are dressed for a day of travel. I don't mean to push you, but the northbound train will leave in an hour."

CHAPTER TWENTY-TWO

Nine train-wracked hours later, Janaczek met us at Station Franz Josef in Prague. Then came the cold, bumpy, three-hour ride in the fumes of an open Graf & Stift Phaeton. By that time, I was crazed from sleep deprivation, but the destination had become clear to me: Konopischt Castle. My tired, overtaxed heart sank. Franzi had purchased the beautiful but crumbling Gothic relic years ago, before we had reunited, and it had just sat there continuing to crumble. I had visited there and was never warm enough for a good night's sleep. I shivered even more as I contemplated padding out on frozen ground to one of the outdoor privies. Franzi sat next to Janeczek while I huddled in misery under furs in the rear seat. I realized that this trip was contrived to punish me for my outburst on the balcony, injury inflicted by a vain husband upon the insult of an even vainer imperial functionary. Archduke Franz Ferdinand was going to lock me away in a castle keep, just like Eleanor of Aquitaine and other marquee wives unwanted by English kings. For this I would change my name back to Perdita. Poor me!

But that's not all. As the crowning malicious act of spoiler-cruelty, my husband managed to ruin my hard-won self-pity.

Footmen opened the front doors to reveal a completely renovated castle radiating warmth. There were vibrant Persian rugs in the foyer. Its walls, now papered in Habsburg black and yellow stripes, shone with sconces of electric light bulbs. A fire crackled in the broad fireplace in the drawing room. The renovated ballroom floor held new parquetry reminiscent of Larisch Palace and the masked ball. Breathtaking Italian masterworks from Franzi's inheritance of the d'Este fortune hung everywhere on the walls.

The kitchen staff served a late supper of piping hot potato and leek soup, grilled weisswurst, chewy black bread, churned butter, mounds of braised red cabbage, and mineral water. The entire staff of butlers, cooks, footmen, maids, gamekeepers, automobile mechanics, and stable boys, entered the dining room from its French doors at the side, two by two, carrying rustic wreaths fashioned from pine boughs, or of straw bound by thin vines and sprigs of orange bittersweet berries. All were presented to me with smiles and heaped at my feet. Janaczek sat on a stool in the corner of the dining hall with his hurdy-gurdy. On an impulse, I rushed to the side of a shy, sixteen-year-old girl from the kitchen wearing clogs, her hair in a two-layered bun. To the hurdy-gurdy's wheezing waltz, she and I improvised a country dance of flirtation.

Following supper, Franzi and Janaczek took me on a tour which included their proud display of eight modern bathrooms with running water and high-tank, brass pull-chain toilets. There was new central heating and even an electric elevator. Finally, Janaczek pointed to one of the tall clocks and suggested we might wish to retire.

I was entirely over the previous contretemps. In our bedchamber that night, I caught Franzi's hand. I drew it to the side of my neck and wedged it there tightly.

"You did not organize all this overnight," I whispered.

"Keen eye for detail, Sophie, as usual," he said with a smile. "Janaczek and I have been about this since the wedding. There's more to finish on the grounds, of course, but I do believe I have a solution to the unpleasantness of Vienna. I brought you here now to consider the plan that I have been working on ever since Montenuovo first started wounding you.

"We have wires into the castle for electricity, the telegraph, and the telephone. With the telegraph and telephone, I will be able to conduct nearly all my business and military duties from Konopischt as my headquarters. I propose we pull up stakes at Belvedere and take up permanent residence here. From here we can travel freely when it suits us, including to Vienna when my presence is required, or when you wish to simply visit or shop. This is compromise, the art of diplomatic life.

"I propose we make this place our home. I'm certain our lives here would be more normal without the torments of Montenuovo. I can certainly work more productively knowing you are happier, as I hope you will be here.

"I don't hate Montenuovo, it's he who hates me. He obviously hates you as well. Do you hate him?"

I said, "He has hurt me and humiliated me. I hate that and I fear him. I can't say I hate him. I want to be where I never have to think about him. You've made such a place. As you say, in this place you could have it both ways: a high royal perch and a down-to-earth family life. I'd be blissfully happy with that if you can really bend your life around it."

Franzi slapped his thigh and said, "There you have it! There are real enemies of the Habsburgs. I need to focus on keeping the peace in the face of them, not one man. Montenuovo has always been just an obstacle. A problem to solve. I simply chose to work on the problem, not the person. We win if we make him irrelevant to us. A crown has always hung over me like the sword of Damocles. When I eventually wear the dangling crown, I will be ready to serve. You, Sophie, are the only woman I have ever loved, and the only woman I have ever known capable of such a life."

FRANZI'S ELEGANT CHOICE DID safeguard our happiness. It was nothing short of pure genius. We left Belvedere and moved to the chambers and halls of Konopischt, with its rose garden, park, lake, and villagers. Franzi's remodeling work had transformed it into the most comfortable and modern country estate in the realm, a hundred-plus miles north of Vienna and thirty-some miles southeast of Prague. "As opposite as night and day" is the overused phrase for ultimate contrasts. Our deeply personal equivalent for "night and day" was "Belvedere and Konopischt."

Oh, and another thing: I was going to have a baby!

Little Sophie arrived seventeen hours after the first labor pains—hours that seemed like years. After the nurse handed her to Franzi, the first person he showed her to was Janaczek!

A year later there was Max, and two years after him came Ernst. They filled our new home and new lives, and fulfilled our oldest dreams. Franzi pampered them. I assigned them chores. Janaczek put them to work in the sheepfold.

CHAPTER TWENTY-THREE

March 25, 1907
Sidonie Zdenka Chotek, Novitiate
Sisters of Sacred Heart
Bregenz, Austria

My dear sister,
Glory! How you must be bursting with emotion in your first year of a new life of service! We ourselves are bursting with pride for you, dear Zennie. Along with my own special happiness for you, I send greetings from Franzi, Little Sophie, Max, and Ernst.

I'm sure you are overwhelmed by all this. I understand your first year will be challenging, but I also know your strong spirit. And now, Easter approaches on top of all the other spiritual riches you have made for yourself.

My own man of peace, as he truly is in his heart, has turned forty-three. Remember how I used to worry that he would have no time for family? How unnecessary that was. He is a full-time father, Zennie, today as much as when he fretted over my labors with our Sophie. I've heard him often say, "My children are my delight and pride." He puts off going into Vienna until it is absolutely required of him and then he returns straight away. He is up early every day and has breakfast in the nursery where he lingers, scrunched up at their small table, until his aide-de-camp comes to drag him away. He prattles on to them about great affairs of state on equal footing and significance as their own squabbles and victories. And he is exceedingly kind to the servants. He insists that the children help them when they can and show them respect in every way.

And now you have gained an entire world of new sisters just by walking through a doorway! I hope your regard for me is not diluted by joining so many who are called to service as you have been. I believe I had a similar experience, which was transformative for me. I know, you think my so-called memories of a past life are my delusions. Fine, I've given up trying to persuade you otherwise, and it doesn't matter at this point. Just know that joining our Chotek family was to me as welcome and heartwarming as you must feel in your new community.

We will all travel to Bregenz during the holidays. Your new family and duties must take precedence, of course, so don't fret about us. We will enjoy any glimpse of you that you can spare. It will be enough for us to simply admire the lake you are on and the mountains that embrace you in your new, storybook village.

With eternal love,

Sophie

I was folding the letter when two arms closed around me under my chin. Before I could turn, I felt a kiss on the nape of my neck. Rather than finish the turn, I lowered my head to rest on his arms, hoping for another kiss.

"Who's that you're writing to?" He did kiss my neck again.

"Oh, it's a letter to Zennie. She must be lonely. She won't say it, but I can tell. I know I would be, no matter how deeply committed."

"Do they still have that thing?"

"What thing?

"You know, the vow thing. That celibacy vow."

I pressed my heels against the floor and pushed back against his chest. "Of course they do. I mean I've never asked her straight out, but those things aren't just temporary. It's been that way for over a thousand years. I think we'd have heard if they'd changed it."

"Come to bed, Sophie."

"Really? I thought you were going somewhere else with that. I thought you might be interested in going celibate."

"I think it's overrated. Come to bed, Sophie."

"You mean that light walnut, Louis XIV bed with Egyptian cotton sheets?"

"That's as I remember it from last night." The arms began to move, as did the hands.

I carefully peeled the arms away from me. "I don't know, Franzi. I'm not so sure."

"Oh, I was hoping. But if you're feeling unwell."

"I feel great," I shrugged.

"So, what is it, Soph? Do you want to try another bed? There are lot to choose from."

"No, not that. Janaczek keeps the Phaeton in what used to be the barn, right?"

"That's right. Did you want to take a drive in the moonlight?"

"No, silly. But, there's a new barn now, isn't there?"

"About twenty meters from the garage. Next to the stock pond. What's on your mind?"

I twisted to face him. He looked puzzled. I continued, "Is there a hayloft in the new barn?"

The puzzled look disappeared. "Yes, there is, Sophie."

"Would there be hay in the new hayloft?"

He pursed his lips judiciously. "Of course, Sophie. That's why it's a hayloft. Might you want to go take a look at the new hayloft tomorrow?"

"Now."

"The hayloft *now*?"

I nodded. I lowered my eyelids. "Would there be barn swallows there?"

Again, he adopted a judicious tone. "Almost certainly. After all it is a barn."

I nodded. "Good point. And, after all, the national bird of Austria is the swallow. Come on, Franzi. Don't be such an archduke. Let's pretend it's the Fold."

The judicious look changed to one more deeply serious. "Sophie, you shouldn't overestimate the ardor of a three-thousand-year-old Mycenaean."

"And you, my dear heart, shouldn't underestimate the allure of a Sicilian girl who grew up on a ranch."

CHAPTER TWENTY-FOUR

One couldn't walk the halls of Konopischt Castle without the anxiety of becoming impaled on the horns of some beast. Franzi and Janaczek hung racks of antlers everywhere, from floor to ceiling. Some of the hallways were narrow, but that never slowed them in their quest to mount herds of wild animal heads and their ominous antlers. In these halls the risk ran high that some exuberant guest, after too many cocktails. might fail to safely navigate the gauntlet. Of course, it never happened, and guests routinely took the spectacle in stride.

Less well known was one particular room that Franzi chose to decorate himself without aid of museum curator or even me. That would be his private, secluded retreat he called the "Saint George Room." It was a room dedicated entirely to the patron saint of, not only England, but Ukraine, Ethiopia, Georgia, Catalonia and Aragon in Spain, Moscow, and half a dozen other places. Franzi hung Saint George flags on the walls in there along with icons, paintings, and kitschy beach-arcade prizes. He also mounted on one wall a glass case holding swords from different eras, starting with a Greek xiphos. He would often go off by himself in the Saint George Room when he wanted to write about his utopian plans for

Europe's Great Powers in a union of common interests and markets. He also liked to meet in there with his closest confidantes after a day of hunting.

As you might expect, the more secretive he kept the Saint George Room, the more curious about it our children became. Little Sophie would hold her nose at the thick cigar smoke that spilled through the crack under the door. It fell to her to herd Max and Ernst away from Franzi's inner sanctum. But, gifted with a very bright mind, she eventually figured out how to get everyone in there at once.

She came to me with an idea for Ernst's tenth birthday. It was very clever. The idea was that the children would "capture" Franzi and march him into the Saint George Room where he would have to tell them a story to be set free. All three of them were in on it. I made sure that it went smoothly by alerting Franzi so he could be thinking about what his story would be.

Ernst's tenth birthday came up on May 27, six months after Franzi turned fifty. The timing was perfect since he and I would travel to Sarajevo just a month later. We opened Ernst's presents at lunch, and the children had gone off to the tennis courts to let him practice with his new racquet. Franzi and I were enjoying quiet tea with Janaczek in the courtyard when the children marauded back through the garden gate. They fell upon Franzi and tugged him through the treacherous hallway of antlers to the locked door of the Saint George Room.

Franzi unlocked the door and we all poured in. It was stuffy, so I pushed open the two lead-mullioned windows through unruly branches of an overgrown yellow apple tree. Franzi gave us a guided tour of his collection of Saint George displays, each depicting the

Roman soldier's brave attack on the dragon which daily had been consuming, first, villagers' sheep, then their children, and ultimately threatened to do the same to the king's maiden daughter. He didn't so much recount the story as reenact it, with all the brio of a one-man theatrical troupe. The children rolled with laughter. They had rarely seen Franzi act so foolishly.

Then he settled himself and began to describe why he had made such a collection. He told them that once upon a time he himself had confronted such a dragon, one with three heads.

"Oh, Papa, we're too old for that," declared Little Sophie.

"Boooo, Papa!" said Ernst, "You can't fool us with that."

Franzi went to the glass case and withdrew the short sword. "Oh, but this is not a prank," he insisted, "I had taken myself to a faraway place where I thought I might never see your mother again. Blocking my return was a three-headed dragon, just like the ones in these pictures and banners. I fought them like a fiend."

He proceeded to swirl the xiphos in the careful, purposeful manner of a trained hoplite. It was then that the children quieted and stared in admiration. Franzi turned, thrust, turned again, parried, dipped, rolled to one side, and rose for another thrust in a choreographed routine that could not have been impromptu play.

Suddenly, Little Sophie let out a terrified, high-pitched shriek. We turned to her. She was pointing to the window. There on the sill lay a coiled snake. Janaczek was on his feet immediately and rushed to the window. The creature turned, writhed back along the tree branch, and down its trunk to disappear into the earth. He said, "Nothing to worry about. It's a common tree adder. They're non-venomous. It's as scared as you are. I've never seen one move so fast. Went straight to ground."

That was welcome news, but the interruption broke the mood completely. The fun was over for the day. Franzi was unsmiling, pale, and subdued, his gaze somewhere far beyond the walls of Konopischt Castle.

EPILOGUE

"If ever a man went anywhere of his own free will, Franz Ferdinand went so to Sarajevo."

—Rebecca West, *Black Lamb and Grey Falcon*

"The emperor left the archduke with no choice."

—King and Woolmans, *The Assassination of the Archduke*

"Free will without fate is no more conceivable than spirit without matter, good without evil."

—Friedrich Nietzsche, *Fatum und Geschtchte*

Call me Peleus or call me Janaczek, I'll simply close with these thoughts. King Agamemnon chose love of duty over love of family, trashed his innocent daughter, and abandoned the rest of his family to wither in the decay of the House of Atreus. Enraged by false jealousy, King Leontes condemned his innocent daughter to death by abandonment in the wilderness. Orestes and Perdita, in the story you saw unfold before your very eyes, escaped their legends by force of sheer will and succeeded completely in their choice of love of family.

Emperor Franz Josef had told the Archduke that, as the army's inspector general, he ought to show the yellow and black flag and the face of the House of Habsburg during maneuvers of the 15th and 16th Corps in Sarajevo on June 28th, 1914. His only official duty would be to preside over a local library opening. It was three days before Franzi and Sophie's fourteenth wedding anniversary.

It was also St. Vitus Day, a Serbian national holiday for sorrow and remembrance of the subjugation of its people by the Ottoman Empire in the late fourteenth century. It was a day that every Serb vowed revenge against foreign rule.

Franzi wanted to go to Sarajevo alone. He told Sophie he had a bad feeling about the trip. He said, "It's better that I go on without you."

She put her foot down. "Absolutely not. I can't bear to watch you go off into the unknown without me! I did that once before and very nearly lost you forever. Besides, the children will be fine with you, won't they, Janaczek?"

Trouble between the empire and Serbia had been brewing over treatment of South Slavs and Orthodox Serbs after the Habsburg Empire took over the kingdom of Serbia from the Ottoman Turks in 1878. Newspaper demands for "Death to Austria" escalated immediately in 1908 when the House of Habsburg annexed Bosnia-Herzegovina outright. When the Archduke's Sarajevo trip was announced, a radical newspaper columnist called for Serbs to "…take up whatever you can: knives, rifles, bombs, or dynamite! Take Holy vengeance! Death to the Habsburg Dynasty."

Bosnian nationalist hotheads bent on revenge poached the Serbian rebel name "Black Hand," and obtained weapons, training, and money in Serbia. But Black Hand's elitist leaders actually had tried to stop the conspiracy; the last thing Serbia needed was a war with a Great Power.

So then, what was the animating revenge? There were anecdotal tales in Sarajevo of fiery bravado among three of the conspirators in a cafe the night before the double assassination. They told of one who shouted, "Beware the Furies dressed as pissed-off peasants, honeybun," but no one paid attention to him…or was it a her? Memories faded and such details were irrevocably lost in the horrific aftermath.

What do we say of the role of fate? Franz Ferdinand was on course to inherit a fully amortized, polyglot empire to govern at a time when its governed were aspiring to constitutions. As Sissi had said, the empire was a cracked egg. Its visible fracture lines were the twelve languages of the realm, with fainter ones along the multiple dialects within each, spoken by fifty million souls who felt stronger cohesions within those segments than across their lines. As fate would have it, he did not repair the egg and he did not break the egg. The egg broke him, Sophie, and everything else this side of the Other Edge.

ABOUT THE AUTHOR

John Feist writes from his home in Falls Church, Virginia. His childhood memories from Kansas led to a literary novel, *The Color of Rain: A Kansas Courtship in Letters*. His experiences as an international business attorney led to The Three Heirs series of four suspense novels. His interest in theatre led to a role in *The Oresteia,* and its characters have haunted him ever since.

OTHER BOOKS BY THE AUTHOR

The Color of Rain: A Kansas Courtship in Letters (Winter Wheat Press, 2021), a literary novel set in 1896-97 and created from the complete courtship correspondence between a widowed banker in Horton, Kansas, and a young schoolteacher in Nortonville, Kansas.

The Three Heirs, a series of eco-disaster suspense thrillers. Three heiresses become entangled with terror plots and Japan's political scene as they juggle high adventure, hectic lives, and new loves. They turn to Brad Oaks to unlock their tangled dilemmas. Brad can solve a global crisis, but can he solve his own solitude? Books in this series include:

> *Night Rain, Tokyo* (Winter Wheat Press, 2019), a pipedream becomes an international fever dream.

> *Blind Trust* (Winter Wheat Press, 2020), the sabotage of her nation's power grid suddenly thrusts Japan's first woman prime minister into a conflict of loyalty between family and country.

> *Doubt and Debt* (Winter Wheat Press, 2021), ruthless, dark-money billionaires turn their greed to the sisters' inheritance.

> *Ship of Perils* (Winter Wheat Press, 2022), a malignant submarine attack plotted on Capitol Hill threatens to sink an unarmed ship on a mission of mercy.

Pocket Japan (Winter Wheat Press, 2021), a concise guidebook and informative approach to conducting business and forming relationships with Japanese business partners.